DEATH BEFORE BEDTIME

In the early fifties novelist Gore Vidal brought his talent and wit to three mysteries under the pseudonym Edgar Box, featuring amateur sleuth Peter Cutler Sargeant II.

Sargeant travels to Washington to handle the press for Senator Leander Rhodes, who is planning to run for the presidency. When he is murdered, Sargeant investigates a locked–room mystery to clear his name and find the real killer.

Originally published by Dutton in 1953, this edition of *Death Before Bedtime* contains a new introduction by the author.

DEATH BEFORE
BEDTIME

EDGAR BOX

THE
ARMCHAIR
DETECTIVE
LIBRARY

Originally published in 1953 by Dutton
Published simultaneously in trade, collector and limited editions
by The Armchair Detective Library in May 1991.
3 5 4 2

ISBN 0-922890-90-0 Trade $18.95
0-922890-91-9 Collector $25
0-922890-92-7 Limited $75

The Armchair Detective Library
129 West 56th Street
New York, New York 10019–3881

Library of Congress Cataloging–in–Publication Data
Box, Edgar, 1925–
Death before bedtime/Edgar Box
p. cm.
Originally published: 1953.
I. Title.
PS3543.I26D36   1991
813'.54—dc20   91–383

Printed in the United States of America

INTRODUCTION

Years ago, there was an advertising slogan: "I got my job through *The New York Times* ", a plug for that paper's Want Ads. As it turned out, I lost mine through *The New York Times*.

In 1943, at seventeen, I enlisted as a private in the Army of the United States, where I served without distinction in the Pacific Theatre of Operations as first mate of an army freight–supply ship. While on watch in port at Dutch Harbor, Aleutian Islands, I wrote a novel called *Williwaw*. In 1946, not yet twenty–one, I was a civilian and a published author.

In those days, the only American book review that mattered was that of the daily *New York Times*. Orville Prescott's praise could establish an author; his dispraise could be terminal; to be ignored by Prescott was not to be.

As earliest of the war–novelists, I was admired by the press, and Prescott's review of *Williwaw* was approving. All was well until my third novel, *The City and the Pillar*. Somehow I had worked out a major American muddle: no one was heterosexual, no one was homosexual. The two made–up words are simply adjectives to describe

i

specific sexual acts, not people. It is significant that neither is a word accepted by semanticists. "Homosexuality" was invented in 1879, a weird coupling of the Greek for "same" and the latin for "sex". The oxford English Dictionary still refuses to accept "heterosexuality", which made its first appearance in the more easy–going *New York Times* in 1930. Before that, sex was presumably, a matter of this and that as opposed to this *or* that.

Orville Prescott was so shocked by my knowledge of Latin and Greek that he told E.P. Dutton that he would never again read, much less review, a novel of mine. In the six years after *The City and the Pillar,* I published five novels. True to the dread Prescott's word, the books were not reviewed in the daily *Times* or by sympathetic *Time* and *Newsweek*. A genre writer needs no reviews to survive but a "literary" one does.

One reason that I like to tell my sad story is that no one believes it. "He claims", journalists sniff as they report on the "alleged" blackout. Even biographers, now gathering like birds of ill–omen on the high branches of one's tree of life, refuse to check whether or not those books were reviewed. But then, in bravery's home, what ought not to be true is not true.

Nevertheless, the United States, in its endearingly half–ass way, was doing its very best to imitate the official enemy of the day, the Soviet Union. Russians literally erased dissidents in their camps. We would erase them with hostile silence, or, if that didn't work, we denied them work altogether. By 1952, the country was loud with loyalty oaths and investigations of Un–American Activities while blacklists of every kind flourished. In historical context my fate was to have been expected. The twin articles of belief of our briefly imperial society were the existence and absolute good of heterosexuality in bed, and the absolute evil of something vaguely known as Communism under the bed. In a world bestseller, I had demonstrated that the first didn't make sense; then, over the years, I came to realize, as did George and Barbara Bush, that the second didn't really mean much of anything either.

Unluckily for individuals, we don't live in historical contexts. We live in a day–to–day present, and it was very odd indeed for a young American to be a respected writer in England, and a hated one at home if the odd—very odd—occasional reviews were anything to go by. Luckily, I was still in my mid–twenties and I was designed by nature for battle. But, first, survival. I had no money, and I could not teach as writers do now because I had never gone to college.

"We have made a fortune with Mickey Spillane," said the elegant creator of Signet–Mentor–New American Library. He and I had been working together on the first of a series of paperback literary anthologies that I had thought up named New World Writing. Since I had got most of the writers for the first issue, I had hoped to become the editor, but that was not possible. The name. *My* name. "Not possible, old boy. But you'll be credited, somehow, don't worry." My sulphurous name finally appeared along with several other names of those who had been helpful. Apparently, I was on a permanent blacklist, all the more deadly because it was nowhere written down. At the Sunday *New York Times Book Review,* my friend, the assistant editor, Harvey Breit, told me, "Why don't you do something else for awhile? Or use a pseudonym."

The elegant Victor Weybright's great luminous frog eyes stared at me over a heavy lunch of frog legs at the Brussels restaurant in New York. He knew the problem of the name. "What we lack is something stylish in the mystery line. Someone like S.S. Van Dine. Perhaps you could . . ." He gave me some unreadable books by Van Dine. As a boy, I had read Agatha Christie, Dorothy Sayers, Dashiell Hammett, but not, alas, Raymond Chandler. I went up the Hudson to my house, and in eight days I wrote *Death in the Fifth Position.* For seven days I wrote a ten thousand word chapter a day; then, on the eighth day, I tidied up.

How did I know so much about ballet? I had been hospitalized at Fort Richardson, Alaska, for exposure, and my knees were arthritic. I had money coming to me from the GI Bill of Rights for a college education, which I didn't want. So I used some of the government funds to take ballet classes to restore my knees.

Victor was delighted. "Do another." I did another and then another, all in the same year, (1952); each took eight days.

The Washington background to *Death Before Bedtime* was that of my youth;I was to return to it, seriously, a dozen years later, in *Washington, D.C.* The relative simplicity of the Hamptons, forty years ago, I have preserved, fondly, in *Death Likes It Hot*. None of the Edgar Box titles is mine.

"We need a name for you, and perfect secrecy." The name Edgar pleased us both. There had been Poe and Wallace. Then, at a party, Victor met a British couple, who were film producers: their name was Box. The rest is history.

Perfect secrecy was maintained for twenty years. The three Edgar Boxes had been printed in more languages than I have. Finally, when Dorothy B. Hughes listed *Death in the Fifth Position* as one of the best, etc.—she blew, as it were, my cover. Shortly after, the editor of an encyclopedia of mystery writers sent me the biography of Box that he intended to publish. I was astonished to read all the pleasant things, unknown to me, the various critics of the genre had written about Edgar Box. But I asked the editor not to include me—him—in his Who's Who as I didn't feel I really belonged. Next, I added, unkindly, you'll be listing Green Hornet radio writers. I was included, of course; but the tributes to Box were dropped.

Despite the passage of cautionary decades, nothing really changes in freedom's land. Each Edgar Box book was exuberantly praised by *The New York Times* crime reviewer, Anthony Boucher. In the wake of Dorothy B. Hughes' revelation, the three Box books were published in a single volume, and Box was revealed, on the cover, to be me. *The New York Times* then denounced the three books that, under another name, *The New York Times* had admired. What's in a name? Now you know.

Thirty years ago, I was trapped in the Athens airport with nothing to read. I went over to the few shelves devoted to paperbacks in English and saw, to my horror, that every book was by me, including the three Boxes. So, for the first time, I read Edgar Box. I found him very funny indeed, and the puzzles properly puzzling, at least to me but then I had forgotten the books—unlike Agatha Christie whose plots I remember vividly after the third chapter; and know despair if it is midnight in a strange city.

Why no more Boxes? Because I moved on to live television drama in 1964; then to the movies and to Broadway; then back to the novel. Today, except for the unfortunate playwright who wants to open in New York, the *Times* no longer carries much weight while the city itself is just another seedy stop on the circuit.

What's Edgar Box like to read now? I think he's still pretty funny. I also think he may now come into his own as what he has become, a historical novelist of the noon–like fifties, when the American empire was at it's peak, and everything worked, and New York City glittered—first city in the world, we called it, and you could be sure—oh, absolutely sure,—if it's Westinghouse, and no one felt the urgent need to implore you in whining voice, to have a nice day now.

Edgar Box
July 30, 1990
(per Gore Vidal)

To V. W.

ONE

I

"I wish I had a drink," she sighed.

"I think you're an alcoholic." I was very severe because Ellen Rhodes is an alcoholic, or at least well on her way to becoming one: but of course her habits are no concern of mine; we are just playmates of the most casual sort.

Ellen was a lovely girl, not yet twenty-five, with only one marriage (annulled at seventeen) to her credit. Her hair was a dirty blond, worn long, and her eyebrows and eyelashes were black, naturally black, and the brows arched. her skin was like ivory, to worry a cliché. . . . I watched her back with some pleasure. I like backs . . . only æsthetically: I mean I don't make a thing of it, being old-fashioned; yet I must say there is nothing that gives me quite such a charge as a female back, especially the double dimple at the base of the spine, the centre of balance a dancer friend of mine once assured me.

"Darling, will you get my bag out from under the bed? the small one? I seem to recall having hidden the better part of a fifth in there just before we left Boston."

"Very provident," I said, disapprovingly, but I got the bottle for her and we both had a drink.

From far away a conductor shouted: "New Haven!"

"Ellen."

She moaned softly, her face entirely covered by hair.

"We're almost there. The train's just leaving Baltimore."

"Oh." She sat up and pushed the hair out of her eyes and blinked sleepily at me.

"I hate men," she said simply.

"Why?"

"I just do." She frowned. "I feel awful. I hate the morning."

" 'Morning in the bowl of night has flung the stone which put the stars to flight. . . .' " I quoted sonorously as we dressed.

"Is that poetry?"

"Indeed it is," I said, pushing up the blind and letting in the cold white light of a December morning. "Picturesque Baltimore," I remarked, as the train passed slowly through that city of small shabby houses with white doorsteps.

"Coffee," said Ellen, sitting down with a thump; she is a miraculously fast dresser for a woman . . . a quality I find both rare and admirable in the opposite sex.

If the waiter thought anything amiss when he served us breakfast in the compartment, he did not betray it; not that I minded particularly, nor for that manner did Ellen . . . rather, I had a job at stake and I didn't want to be caught in a compromising position with the daughter of my new client, the incomparable, the reactionary Senator Leander Rhodes, the only adult American male to be called Rhodes without the inevitable nickname Dusty.

"Now I feel better," said Ellen, after she'd finished two cups of black coffee, the alcoholic fumes of the night before dispelled.

In the year that I had known her she was either just coming out from under a hang-over or else going into one, with a moment or two, I suppose, of utter delight when she was in between, when she was high. In spite of the drinking, however, I liked her. For several years she had been living in New York, travelling with a very fast set of post-debutantes and pre-alcoholics, a group I occasionally saw at night clubs or the theatre, but nowhere else.

I am a hard-working public relations man with very little time for that kind of living. I would never have met Ellen if she hadn't been engaged for eight weeks last year to a class-mate of mine from Harvard. When the eight blissful weeks of engagement to this youth were up, she was engaged to me for nearly a month; I was succeeded then, variously, by a sleek creature from the Argentine, by a middle-aged novelist, and by a platoon of college boys to each of whom she was affianced at one time or another and, occasionally, in several instances, at the same time. Not that she is a nymph. Far from it. She just likes a good time and numerous engagements seem to her the surest way of having one.

"Won't Father be surprised to see us together!" she said at last.

"Yes." I was a little worried. I had never met Senator Rhodes. I had been hired by his secretary who had, I was quite sure, known nothing about my acquaintance with Ellen. My contract with the Senator was to run three months with an option in March and then another after that . . . by which time, if I were still on the job, the National Convention would be meeting and the Mid-West's favourite son, Lee Rhodes, would go before the convention as the people's choice for President of the United States, or so I figured it, or rather so I figured Senator Rhodes figured it. Well, it was a wonderful break for the public relations firm of Peter Cutler Sargeant II, which is me.

Ellen had been more cynical about it when I told her the news in Cambridge, where we had been attending a Harvard function. In spite of her cynicism, however, we had both decided, late at night, that it would be a wonder-

3

ful idea if we went straight to Washington from Boston, together, and surprised the Senator. It had all seemed like a marvellous idea after eight Martinis, but now, in the cold light of a Maryland morning, I was doubtful. For all I knew the Senator loathed his daughter, paid her liberally to keep out of Washington . . . nervously, I recalled some of Ellen's exploits: the time last spring when she undressed beneath a full moon and went swimming in the fountain in front of the Plaza Hotel in New York, shouting: "I'm coming, Scottie . . . Zelda's coming!" in imitation of that season's revival Scott Fitzgerald . . . imposing on the decorous 1950s the studied madness of the 1920s. Fortunately, two sober youths got her out of there before the police or the reporters discovered her.

"What do you think your father's up to?" I asked, resigned to my fate: it was too late now to worry about the Senator's reaction to this combination.

"Darling, you know I hate politics," she said, straightening one eyebrow in the window as frame houses and evergreens flashed by.

"Well, he must be planning something. I mean, why hire a Press agent like me?"

"I suppose he's going to run for the Senate again."

"He was re-elected last year."

"I suppose he was. Do let's send George and Alice a wire, something funny . . . they'll die laughing when they hear we're on a train together."

"You know I think it's quite wonderful your father's done as well as he has, considering the handicap a daughter like you must be to him."

Ellen chuckled. "Now that's unkind. As a matter of fact, he simply adores me. I even campaigned for him when I was fifteen years old. Made speeches to the Girl Scouts from one end of the state to the other. . . . I even

4

spoke to the Boy Scouts, lovely young creatures. There was one in Talisman City, an Eagle Scout with more . . ."

"I don't want to hear any of your obscene reminiscences."

She laughed. "You *are* evil, Peter. I was just going to say that he had more Merit Badges than any other scout in the Mid-West."

"I wonder if he's running for President."

"I don't think he's old enough. You have to be thirty-five, don't you? That was ten years ago and he was seventeen then, which would make him . . . how old now? I could never add."

"I was referring to your father, not that Eagle Scout of infamous memory."

"Oh, Daddy. Well, I don't know." Ellen was vague. "I hope not."

"Why not?"

"It's such a bore. Look at the time poor Margaret Truman had, trailed by detectives and guards everywhere."

"If you were a nice girl like Miss Truman you wouldn't mind."

"Oh . . . !" And Ellen Rhodes said a bad word.

"There would be all sorts of compensations, though," I said, trying to look on the bright side. "I think it would be very pleasant having a father who was President."

"Well, I don't. Besides, I don't think Mother will let him run. She's always wanted to go back to Talisman City, where we came from originally."

"That would be nice for you."

Ellen snorted. "I'm a free spirit," she said, and, all things considered, she was, too.

We parted at the Union Station. Ellen went home in a cab and I walked across the square to the Senate Office Building, a white cake of a building in the shadow of the Capitol.

Senator Rhodes's office was in a corner on the first floor, attesting to his seniority and power since he was, among other things, Chairman of the Spoils and Patronage Committee.

I opened the door of his office and walked into a high-ceilinged waiting-room with a desk and receptionist at one end. Several petitioners were seated on the black leather couches by the door. I told the woman at the desk who I was, and she immediately told me to go into the Senator's office, a room on the left.

The room was empty. It was a fascinating place, and while I waited I examined everything: the vast mahogany desk covered with party symbols, the hundreds of photographs in black frames on the wall: every important political figure since 1912, the year Leander Rhodes came to the Senate, was represented. Leather chairs were placed around a fireplace on whose mantel were arranged trophies and plaques, recording political victories . . . while above the mantel was a large political cartoon of the Senator, handsomely framed. It showed him, his shock of grey unruly hair streaming in the wind of Public Opinion, mounted upon a spavined horse called Political Principle.

"That was done in 1925," said a voice behind me.

I turned around quickly, expecting to find the Senator. Instead, however, a small fat man in grey tweed, wearing owl-like spectacles, stood with hand outstretched, beaming at me. "I'm Rufus Hollister," he said as we shook hands. "Senator Rhodes's secretary."

"We've had some correspondence," I said.

"Yes, sir, I should say so. The Senator's over in the Capitol right now . . . important vote coming up this morning. But sit down for a minute before we join him and let's get acquainted."

We sat down in the deep arm-chairs. Mr. Hollister smiled, revealing a handsome upper plate. "I suspect," he said, "that you're wondering exactly why I engaged you."

"I thought Senator Rhodes engaged me."

"He did, he did, of course . . . I was speaking only as his . . . proxy, as it were." He smiled again, plumply. I decided that I disliked him, but then I usually dislike all men on first meeting: something to do, I suppose, with the natural killer instinct of the male. I tried to imagine Mr. Hollister and myself covered with the skins of wild beasts, doing battle in the jungle, but my imagination faltered: after all, we were two Americans living in rooms centrally heated and eating hygienically prepared food got out of cans . . . the jungle was remote.

"In any case," Hollister was saying, "I thought I should brief you a little before you meet the Senator." He paused. Then he asked: "What, by the way, are your politics?"

Being venal, I said that I belonged to the same party as my employer; as a matter of fact, I have never voted so; even if I did not entirely admire the party of Senator Rhodes I hadn't perjured myself.

Mr. Hollister looked relieved. "I don't suppose, in your business, that you're much interested in politics."

I said that, aside from my subscription to *Time* magazine, I was indeed cut off from the great world.

"You don't have, then, any particular choice for the nominating convention?"

"No, sir, I do not."

"You realise that what I tell you now is in the strictest, the very strictest confidence?"

"I do." I wondered whether or not I should cross my heart; Mr. Hollister had grown strangely solemn and mysterious.

"Then, Mr. Sargeant, as you may already have guessed, The Senator's Hat Is In The Ring."

"The what?"

"Senator Rhodes will announce his candidacy for the nomination for President on Friday at a speech before the National Margarine Council."

I took this awesome news calmly. "And I am to handle the publicity?"

"That's right." He looked at me sharply, but my Irish, piggish features were impassive: I saw myself already as Press Secretary to President Rhodes: "Boys, I've got a big story for you. One hour ago the President laid the biggest egg. . . ." but I recalled myself quickly to reality. Mr. Hollister wanted to know my opinion of Leander Rhodes.

"I hardly have one," I said. "He's just another Senator as far as I'm concerned."

"We, here in the office, regard this as something of a crusade," said Mr. Hollister softly.

"Then I will, too," I said sincerely. Before he could tell me why the country needed Lee Rhodes, I remarked that I happened to know his daughter, that, by chance, I had come down on the train with her. Was it my imagination, as they used to say in Victorian novels, or did a cloud cross Mr. Hollister's serene countenance? As a matter of fact, it was worse than a cloud: it was a scowl.

"Is Miss Rhodes *in* Washington?"

"I believe so. Unless she decided to go back to New York."

"A charming young lady," said Mr. Hollister, without

conviction. "I've known her since she was a tiny tot." The idea of Ellen Rhodes as a tiny tot was ludicrous, but I was not allowed to meditate on it. Instead I was whisked out of the office and into the reception-room; then into a farther office filled with grey women answering the Senator's voluminous mail. I was introduced to all of them; next, I was shown an empty desk which I could call my own, close by one of the tall windows which overlooked the Capitol. I noticed that none of the typists was under fifty, a tribute, I decided, to Mrs. Senator Rhodes.

"Now if you like, we'll go over to the Senate."

I had never been inside either the Senate Office Building or the Capitol before, and so I am afraid that I gaped like a visitor from Talisman City at the private subway which whisked the Senators in little cars from the basement of their building to that of the Capitol.

After we got off a crowded elevator, Mr. Hollister led me down a long marble corridor to a green frosted double glass door beside which stood a uniformed guard. "That's the floor of the Chamber," said my escort, in a low reverent voice. "Now I'll see if I can get you into the cloakroom."

As I later discovered, this was the holy of holies of the Senate, almost as inaccessible to a non-Senatorial visitor as the floor itself. Some quick talk got us in, however.

The cloakroom was a long room with desks, couches and a painted ceiling, very ornate, a little like Versailles: swinging glass doors communicated directly with the Senate Chamber, from which could be heard a loud monotonous voice.

"Senator Rhodes," whispered Mr. Hollister proudly pushing me back against the wall, out of the way of the statesmen who wandered in and out, some chatting together in small groups, others reading newspapers or writing letters. It was like a club, I thought, trying to summon up a little awe, trying to remember that these were the men who governed the most powerful country in the world.

Mr. Hollister pointed out several landmarks: Senator O'Mahoney, Senator Douglas, Senator Byrd . . . I stared at them all. Then the swinging door opened and Leander Rhodes, the Great Bear of the West as he liked to hear himself referred to, appeared in the cloakroom, his face red from speech-making, his grey hair tangled above his blood-shot eyes, eyes like his daughter's, I thought, recalling irreverently her face on the pillow beside me that morning. But no time for that.

"Ah, Sargeant. Glad to see you. Glad to see you. Prompt. I like promptness. Secret of success, punctuality." Since neither of us could either prove or disprove this state-ment, I murmured agreement

"Been to the office yet? Yes? Good scout. Let's go to lunch."

It took us quite a while to get from the cloakroom to the Senate Dining-Room. Every few yards or so, the Senator would pause to shake hands with some other Senator or with some tourist who wanted to meet him. He was obviously quite popular with the voters; the other Senators were a bit cool with him, or so I thought, since he was, after all, by reputation anyway, a near-idiot with a perfect Senate record of obstruction. He regarded the administra-tion of Chester A. Arthur as the high point of American history, and he felt it his duty to check as much as possible the subsequent national decline from that high level. He was a devout isolationist, although, according to legend, at the time of the First World War he had campaigned furiously for our entry into that war, on the side of the Kaiser.

I suppose I shouldn't, in actual fact, accept jobs from men for whom I have so little respect, but since it never occurred to me that Lee Rhodes had a chance in the world of getting nominated, much less elected, President, I saw no harm in spending a few months at a considerable salary to see that his name appeared in the newspaper, often and favourably. The lunch was excellent, served in an old-fashioned dining-room with tile floor where the Senators eat . . . there is a Pre-Civil War feeling about the Senate Dining-Room . . . especially the menu, the remarkable cornbread, the legendary bean soup which I wolfed hungrily, trying not to stare too hard at Senator Taft, who sat demurely at the next table reading a newspaper as he lunched.

"Suppose Rufus here has briefed you?" said Senator Rhodes, when coffee arrived and all around the room cigars were lit, like Roman candles.

I nodded, holding my breath as a wreath of blue Senatorial smoke crossed the table and settled about my neck.

"Day after tomorrow, Friday, that's the big day. Making announcement then. Want it well covered. Can you do that?"

I told him that all speeches by such a celebrated statesman were well covered by the Press. He took my remark quietly, adding that he wanted *Life* there, or else. I said that *Life* would be there.

"Got yourself located yet?" he asked, after we had exchanged a number of very business-like remarks. I said that I hadn't, that I'd only just arrived on the morning train.

"Stay with *us* then; for a few days," said the Senator generously. "Got plenty of room. Give us a chance to talk strategy."

" I'd appreciate that, sir. By the way, I happen to know your daughter slightly. I came down on the train with her this morning."

Was it my imagination . . . no, it wasn't; the Senator sighed rather sadly. "A wonderful girl, Ellen," he said mechanically.

"She seems very pleasant."

"Like her mother . . . a wonderful woman."

"So I've been told."

The Senator rose. "I'll see you this evening then, at the house. Got a committee meeting now. Rufus will show you around. Remember: this is a kind of crusade."

3

A crusade was putting it lightly. It was an unscrupulous and desperate effort of one Leander Rhodes to organise the ill-liberal minority of the country into a party within his party . . . and, I suspect, if he'd been younger and a little more intelligent he might very well have got himself into the White House. As it was, from what little Rufus Hollister would tell me, the Senator had some impressive backing; he also had some very sinister backing. I disguised my alarm, though, and by the time I took a taxi to the Senator's house on Massachusetts Avenue, Mr. Hollister was convinced that I too was a crusader for Good Government and True-Blue American Ideals.

The house on Massachusetts Avenue was an heroic imitation of an Italian villa, covered with yellow stucco and decorated with twisted columns and ironwork balconies. The Senator, I soon discovered, was a very wealthy man, though the source of his income was not entirely clear to me. Mr. Hollister spoke vaguely of properties in Talisman City.

A butler showed me to my room on the third floor and, as I went up the marble staircase, I caught an occasional glimpse of ballrooms, of parquet floors, of potted palms, all very 1920 Grand Hotel *chic*. Dinner would be announced in an hour, I was told. Then I was left alone in a comfortable bedroom overlooking the Avenue.

I was dozing blissfully in a hot bath, when Ellen marched into the bathroom.

"I've come to scrub your back," she said briskly.

"No, you don't," I said, modestly covering myself. "Go away."

"That's hardly the way for my fiancé to act," she said, sitting down on the toilet seat.

"I haven't been your fiancé for almost a year," I said austerely. "Besides, the bride-to-be is not supposed to inspect her groom before the wedding."

"You give me a pain," said Ellen, lighting a cigarette. She wore a very dashing pair of evening pyjamas, green with gold thread, quite Oriental-looking . . . it made her look faintly exotic, not at all like a simple girl from Talisman City. "By the way, I told Mother we were engaged. I hope you don't mind."

I moaned. "What is this allergy you have to the truth?"

"Well, it *was* the truth a few months ago . . . I mean time's relative and all that," she beamed at me. "Anyway, it should help you with my father."

"I'm not so sure," I said, recalling the Senator's look of pain at the mention of his only daughter.

"The house is full, by the way," said Ellen, exhaling smoke. "Some of the dreariest political creatures these old eyes have seen in many a moon."

"Constituents?"

"I suppose so. One's rather sweet . . . a lovely boy from New York, a newspaper-man. He's doing a profile of Father for some magazine, very Left Wing I gather, and of course poor Father doesn't have the remotest notion that he's being taken for a ride. Did you ever see the piece the *Nation* did on him?"

I said that I hadn't; I asked her the name of the lovely boy who was doing the profile. "Walter Langdon . . . a real dream. I had a quick drink with him in the drawing-room, before I dashed off to make violent love to my prospective groom."

"I have a feeling that our engagement isn't going to last very long."

"You may be right. Oh, and you'll never guess who's here . . . Verbena Pruitt."

"My God!" I was alarmed. Anyone would be alarmed at meeting the incomparable Verbena, the President of the Daughters of the War of 1812 as well as National Committee-woman for her party, one of the most powerful lady politicos in the country.

"She's from Daddy's state, you know. She has the hairiest legs I've seen since that football game at Cambridge last week."

"I had better get myself a hotel room quick," I said, letting the bath-water out and standing up, my back turned modestly towards Ellen as I dried myself.

"How do you keep so slim?" asked the insatiable Ellen.

"No exercise is the secret," I said, flexing a muscle or two in an excess of male spirits as I dressed.

"Then there's an old buddy of Father's staying here, Roger Pomeroy and his wife, a poisonous creature. I don't know what *they're* doing here. He's an industrialist back in Talisman City, makes gunpowder or something like that. . . ."

"Sounds like a chummy gathering."

"Grim . . . awfully grim. That tiresome Rufus Hollister, Father's secretary, also lives in. I have often said that he was the reason I left home. Did you ever feel his hands?

Like an uncooked fillet of sole . . . which reminds me I'm hungry, which also reminds me I desperately need a drink. Do hurry . . . here, let me tie your tie . . . I love tying a man's tie: gives me such a sense of power when I think with just the slightest pressure I could choke him to death."

"Darling, have you ever been analysed?"

"Of course. Hasn't everyone? I went every day for three years after my annulment . . . Mother insisted. When it was over I was completely normal; I had passed my course with flying colours: no more inhibitions, no frustrations, an easy conscience about alcohol as well as the slightly decrepit body of a middle-aged analyst named Breitbach added to my gallery of conquests." She finished tying my tie with a flourish which made me jump. "There! You look such a lamb."

4

The drawing-room was a large draughty affair with french windows which looked out on a bleak garden of formal boxwood hedges and empty flower-beds, black with winter. Several people were seated about the fire. Two men rose at our entrance. A woman in black lace rose, too, and approached us. It was Mrs. Leander Rhodes.

"Mother, I want you to meet my fiancé, Peter Sargeant."

"I'm so happy to see you, Mr. Sargeant. I've heard such a great deal about you . . . such a coincidence, too . . . the Senator engaging you without knowing about you and Ellen." She was an amiable-looking woman of fifty, thin and rather bent with, as far as I could tell through the swatches of black lace, no bosom and no waist. At her throat old-fashioned yellow diamonds gleamed. Her eyes were black; only her wide full mouth was like her daughter's. "Let me introduce you around," she said; and she did.

Verbena Pruitt was worse than I'd expected: a massive woman in mauve satin with henna-dyed hair, bobbed short over a red fat neck, large features, small pig eyes and a complexion not unlike the craters of the moon as seen through a telescope. She gave my hand a vigorous squeeze. So did Roger Pomeroy, a tall, silver-haired man of distinction. His wife, Camilla, a fairly pretty dark woman, smiled at me winningly, one heavily veined hand at her smooth neck, fondling pearls. Ellen's lovely boy Walter Langdon, a red-haired youth, mumbled something incoherent as we shook hands. He was obviously uncomfortable. And well he should be, I thought righteously, coming into a man's house like this with every intention of axing him later in a magazine.

"The Senator and Rufus should be along soon," said Mrs. Rhodes, as a maid brought Martinis. Ellen gulped one quickly, like a conjurer; then she took another off the tray and held it in one hand, occasionally sipping it in a most lady-like way. Whom was she trying to impress, I wondered. The lovely boy? or her mother? or the assorted politicos?

At first, I thought that possibly I was the one who was ill at ease, but, by the time dinner was over and we were all seated in the drawing-room having coffee beneath a virile painting of Senator Rhodes, I decided that something was obviously going all wrong, and I surmised that it had to do with Ellen's unexpected visit to Washington. Yet she was a perfect lady all evening. She was a trifle high by the time dinner was over, but she spoke hardly at all . . . in fact, I'd never before seen her so restrained. The Senator was in good form, but I had a feeling that the funny stories

16

he told, and his loud rasping laughter were mechanical, a part of the paraphernalia of public office rather than sincere good spirits. He eyed Ellen and myself suspiciously all evening, and I began to wonder just how long my job was going to last. I cursed Ellen to myself, fervently, furiously . . . her announcement that we were engaged had messed up everything.

The other guests seemed uneasy, except for Verbena Pruitt, who matched the Senator laugh for laugh, joke for joke in a booming political voice.

Brandy was served with coffee and Senator Rhodes, turning to Roger Pomeroy, whom he had ignored most of the evening, said: "Got some good cigars in the study. Want one?"

'No, thank you, Lee,' said the other. "I've had to give up the habit . . . heart."

"None of us are getting any younger!" snorted Miss Pruitt over her brandy, a hairpin falling softly to the carpet. . . . His eye is on the hairpin, I thought irreverently.

"I'm sound as a bell," said the Senator, striking his chest a careful blow. He did not look very sound, though. I noticed how pale he was, how one eyelid twitched, how his hands shook as he lighted a cigar for himself. He was an old man.

"The Senator has the stamina of ten men," said little Sir Echo, Rufus Hollister, smugly.

"He'll need it, too, if he's going after that nomination," said Miss Pruitt with a wink. "Won't you, Lee?"

"Now who told you I was interested in the nomination?" said Senator Rhodes, with an attempt at roguishness, not much of an attempt at that; he was obviously paying very little attention to us. He seemed preoccupied with some perplexing problem. His grey eyes looked unfocused.

While Verbena Pruitt and the Senator sparred, I talked to Mrs. Pomeroy, who sat beside me on the couch. "Such a marvellous man, the Senator," she said, her eyes glowing. "Have you known him long?" I shook my head, explaining my presence in the house.

"We've known the Rhodeses for just years, back in Talisman City. Were you ever there? No? It's a wonderful *residential* town, almost Southern in a way, if you know what I mean. Except we're getting quite a bit of industry there . . . my *husband* is in industry."

"That's very nice," I said.

"We have a *government* contract," said Mrs. Pomeroy importantly. She chattered on about herself, about their home town, about the gunpowder business, about the latest developments in gunpowder: the new process Pomeroy Inc. had developed. While she talked I watched Ellen making time with lovely boy Langdon on the couch opposite us. She was talking to him in a low voice, and I could tell by the gleam in her eyes and the flush of confusion on his youthful puppy-dog face that before this night was over he would be forced to revise his estimate of the Rhodes family since, I was quite confident, long before Aurora showed her rosy head in the east, he would be engaged to the daughter of the house. He was a gone goose . . . for a few weeks, anyway. I wondered if Mrs. Rhodes was on to her daughter. If she was, she hardly showed it. She completely ignored her, speaking for the most part to Mr. Pomeroy and Rufus Hollister, who sat on either side of her, their voices pitched a register below those of Senator Rhodes and Miss Pruitt, who were now speaking of various scandals attendant upon the Denver Convention of 1908.

Just before midnight, Mrs. Rhodes stood up and announced that she was going to bed, but that the others should take no notice of her if they wanted to remain up. "Good nights" were said and the hour for breakfast set. I

18

was wondering whether I should go straight up to bed or wait for some sign from Ellen, when the Senator beckoned to me. "Like to have a little chat with you," he said. "We can go up to my study." I said good-night to everyone. Ellen hardly noticed us go; she was already beginning to unravel poor Langdon, right there on the couch . . . all very lady-like, though: only an experienced eye like mine could tell what she was up to.

The Senator's study was a corner room on the second floor with windows on two sides, oak panelling and book-cases filled with law books (which looked unopened), bound copies of the *Congressional Record* (fairly worn), and thick scrap-books of newspaper clippings, much used, dating from 1912. There were photographs on the walls . . . less political, however, than those in his office. Photographs of his family at various moments in their lives . . . even one of Ellen as a bride. This surprised me since, as I remembered the story, she had eloped with an undesirable and had been brought home before, in the eyes of the law at least, he had soiled her.

The Senator seated himself at a desk in front of the windows. I sat down in a leather arm-chair beside the un-lit fireplace; the room was chilly, I thought. I remember shivering.

"I must tell you frankly," said the Senator, looking at me severely, "that I didn't anticipate this . . . situation."

"What situation?" I acted innocent.

"This business with my daughter . . . this 'engagement'."

"Sir, there is no business with your daughter," I said, sitting up very straight.

"What do you mean, sir?" He was obviously going to out-courtesy me; our manners became more and more ante-bellum. "My daughter gave me to understand that you and she were to be married."

19

"She is mistaken," I said; the job was over, I decided sadly.

"You mean that you refuse, sir, to marry my daughter?"

"I mean, Senator," said I, suddenly weary of the whole farce, "that I have never in my one year's acquaintance with your daughter thought of marrying her nor has she ever thought of marrying me."

He looked at me as though I were Drew Pearson investigating the inner working of the Senate Committee on Spoils and Patronage. He blustered. "Do you mean to imply my daughter is a liar?"

"You know perfectly well what she is," I snapped.

Leander Rhodes sagged in his chair; he looked a hundred years old at that moment. "Young man," he said huskily, "I have misjudged you. I apologise."

"It's nothing, sir," I mumbled. I felt genuinely sorry for the old bastard. He sighed heavily; then he lit another cigar.

"I'll tell you a little about the coming campaign," he said. I was enormously relieved: I wasn't fired after all. "On Friday I shall announce my candidacy. So far the only two candidates officially in the field are both Conservatives . . . neither is quite so Conservative as I am, however, and neither has my following in the Mid-West, among the farmers and small business people. Now I have been in this game long enough to know that high ideals are not enough if you want high office: you have to compromise to win and I want to win and I am willing to compromise with both Labour and the Left Wing, two elements which have never supported me before. You follow me?"

I said that I did, perfectly. I was beginning to revise my estimate of him. He was not entirely a fool. Had he been in the fashionable liberal camp I should probably have thought well of him . . . there were men far less astute than he who enjoyed a good deal more esteem.

"Now I anticipate a deadlock at the convention. . . ." For the next few minutes I was told political secrets which any Washington journalist would have given an arm to know. I found out what the President was going to do and what was going on in the inner circles of both parties . . . it was all very grand. "I am taking you into my confidence young man, because unless you're up on the facts you'll be of no use to me, and you have a lot of work to do. Fortunately, we have money. I am backed in this by some of the richest men in America and we'll spend all the law'll allow . . . and then some." He smiled for the first time since I'd met him: long yellow teeth like a dog's. . . .

It was almost one-thirty when our conference ended. "I feel we understand each other," said the Senator, shaking my hand as he led me to the door.

"I do, too, sir," I said sincerely, not adding, however, that I understood Leander Rhodes so well that I was tempted to take the next train back to New York and start a crusade against him. I had not realised the extent of his cunning nor had I suspected he had so many large sinister interests behind him. It was a chilling interview, even for a political innocent like myself: I realised, as I walked down the hall, that Huey Long had been a ward heeler compared to Senator Rhodes.

In my confusion, I went downstairs to the drawing-room instead of upstairs to my bedroom. The butler was still up, to my surprise, collecting the remains of the coffee-cups and brandy-glasses. He looked at me expectantly but I only smiled vaguely at him and then, seeing a packet of cigarettes on the couch opposite me, I walked over and picked them up, determinedly, as though I had come downstairs for them. The butler and his tray vanished. I stood for a moment, looking into the coals of the fire. The phrase 'Man on horseback' kept going through my head. What a terrible man he was! I though impotently, and what should I do? just how far from virtue should self-interest propel one? It was very perplexing.

"Oh, you gave me a start," said a female voice.

I jumped myself; it was Verbena Pruitt in a dressing-gown of flesh-coloured silk, a vast tent-like affair which made her seem more than ever like a mountain of festering flesh; her thin grey hair was done in paper curlers and I noticed that she had a bald spot the size of a Cardinal's cap on the back of her head.

"I was looking for my cigarettes," said the apparition. "I thought I left them on the couch over there."

I felt like a thief: the lady's cigarettes in my coat pocket. Had I been of strong character, I should have admitted guilt and handed them over to her. But, as usual, I took the easy way. "Perhaps they fell down behind the cushions," I said and I began to search for them with great stage gestures, scrutinising the backs of cushions with an idiot stare.

"It's unimportant," said Verbena Pruitt. "The butler probably took them. They always do. Anything they can get their hands on." She glanced thoughtfully at the row of bottles on a tray near the fireplace.

"Can I get you anything?" I asked eagerly.

"Perhaps a mouthful of that brandy," said Miss Pruitt smiling; I noticed with alarm that her upper teeth had been removed for the night . . . so richly fat was her face, though, that it made hardly any difference. Only her speech was somewhat impaired. I wondered if I should attempt some pleasantry or not about the mouthful . . . did she want me to carry it to her in *my* mouth? I let it go. The Verbena Pruitts of the world were, as far as I was concerned, an unknown and dangerous quantity, capable of any madness. I brought her a stiff shot of brandy, and one for myself.

"That *is* nice," she said, tossing off half of it in such haste that a bit of the essence trickled down her tiers of chins, like Victoria Falls.

We sat down on one of the couches. I could hardly believe it. Here I was alone at night in an empty drawing-room with the First Lady of her Party seated beside me, wearing an intimate garment of the night, her hair in curlers and her teeth waiting for her upstairs in one of the bedrooms. It was the sort of moment every boy dreams of, in nightmares.

"Tell me, my dear young man, what your function is . . . in relation to Senator Rhodes."

"I am to handle his publicity."

"Not an easy job," said Miss Pruitt cryptically, touching her bald spot bemusedly with a hand like a bloated starfish.

"I'm afraid not."

"Lee has many enemies."

"I can see why."

"You what?"

"I mean I can see why . . . considering the principles he stands for and so on," I extemporised hastily.

"Of course. Still most of the press is against him . . . I can't think why except you know what smart alecks those newspaper people are . . . just between you and me and the lamp-post. . . . I hope you won't quote me." She smiled terribly.

"I know what you mean," I said, averting my eyes.

"Lee has such courage," she added irrelevantly, sniffing her brandy like a terrier at a rat's hole. "Take tonight. He actually thinks he can win over that young Communist from New York who's writing a piece about him. He is fearless . . . but he should keep people like that at a distance."

"Perhaps the Senator needs someone to save him from himself," I suggested.

"How right you are, Mr. Schroeder."

"Sargeant."

"I mean Mr. Sargeant. Then you must remember that I'm not exactly *pro*-Rhodes." This last information was given with a shrewd wink which struck me as being oddly unpleasant.

"I thought you were on his committee." Rhodes had given me to understand that Miss Pruitt would deliver the women of America on Election Day.

"Wheels within wheels," said Verbena Pruitt rising to her feet. "But now I must be off to my beauty sleep." And, like Lady Macbeth, she sailed out of the room.

I finished off my brandy slowly. Then, wondering whether or not I should look in on Ellen, I walked up the dimly lit staircase. I was just recalling that I had no idea where her bedroom was when a figure stepped out of the shadows on the first landing. I gave a jump.

"Hope I didn't startle you," said Rufus Hollister smoothly, emerging from the darkened doorway, where he had been standing, into the faint lamplight. He was still dressed.

"Not at all," I said.

"The Senator just phoned me . . . on the house phone. He's working late . . . never lets up . . . secret of his success . . . nose to the grindstone." I was pelted with saws.

"I'll see you in the morning," I said, edging away. I didn't get very far, though. The next thing I knew I was

24

on the floor, in Mr. Hollister's arms, an enormous gold-framed mirror in fragments about us as the whole house rocked back and forth while a sound like thunder or the atomic bomb deafened us and put out all the lights.

They picked a fine moment to bomb Washington was my first conscious thought. My second thought was to check myself in the dark for broken bones. I was all in one piece, I decided, though my cheek was bleeding . . . from the broken glass. Then the shouts and shrieks began. I heard Mr. Hollister cursing in the dark near me, heard the tinkle of glass as he got to his feet and brushed himself off. Then, from all directions, candles appeared, held by servants, by Mrs. Rhodes, By Miss Pruitt, who was standing in the corridor with the Pomeroys. No one knew what had happened. Not until an hour later did we find out, when a police official addressed us in the drawing-room.

It was a curious scene.

A dozen candelabras cast a cool yellow light over the room, making long shadows on the floor. The house party and the servants, in various states of dress and undress, sat in a circle about the police lieutenant, a young man named Winters who stood sternly between two uniformed policemen and surveyed his audience.

"In the first place," he said glaring for some inexplicable reason at Verbena Pruitt, "Senator Rhodes is dead." Mrs. Rhodes, who had already been informed, sat very straight in her chair, her face expressionless. Ellen sat beside her, her eyes shut. The others looked stunned by what had happened. And what *had* happened?

"Some time between nine o'clock yesterday morning and one-thirty-six this morning, a small container of a special new explosive, Pomeroy 5-X, was hidden behind some logs in the fireplace of the Senator's study." There was a gasp.

25

Ellen opened her eyes very wide. Mr. Pomeroy stirred uneasily; his wife chewed her lip nervously. Verbena Pruitt was nearly as impassive as Mrs. Rhodes: she had been through too many political battles to be unnerved by such a small thing as murder, and it *was* murder in the eyes of Lieutenant Winters.

"It is our belief that someone who was closely acquainted with the Senator's habits knew that he usually went to his study alone after dinner to work, and that he always lit his own fire on cold nights. In fact, according to Mrs. Rhodes and the butler here, he was very particular about this fire, insisting that it be made like an Indian tepee of ash logs and strips of pine kindling. It was never lighted by anyone except himself and, in the morning, the coals were always taken out by one of the maids. Yesterday morning they were removed at nine o'clock by . . . " Lieutenant Winters squinted in the candlelight at a sheet of paper he was holding in his hand, "by Madge Peabody, a maid. Fifteen minutes later the butler, Herman Howells, laid the fire. From that moment until Senator Rhodes retired to his study the library was visited by no one . . . except the murderer." Lieutenant Winters paused dramatically and peered through the gloom of candles at his captive audience, unconscious of his errors. I wondered if he'd ever thought of television for a career; with that handsome dull profile, that hypnotic voice he could write his own ticket. I was suddenly very tired; I wanted to go to bed.

Mr. Hollister provided a mild diversion. "And myself," he said calmly. "I was in the study shortly before dinner, at the Senator's request." I held *my* fire.

"I will get your testimony later," said the Lieutenant, a little sharply I thought. His great moment was robbed of some of its drama. He then told us that we were, none of us, to leave the house without police permission. Then, beginning with the ladies, the interviews began. They were held in the dining-room. The rest of us remained in the drawing-room, talking in hushed voices of what had happened, and drinking nervously. Mrs. Rhodes was the first to be interviewed; which was fortunate since her presence embarrassed us all. When she was gone, I was surprised at how calmly the guests took this sudden, extraordinary turn in their affairs . . . especially Ellen who was the coolest of the lot.

"Do fix me a Scotch," she said, while I was standing by the bar getting more brandy for Miss Pruitt. When I had finished my bar duties, I sat beside Ellen on an uncomfortable love-seat. Across the room Miss Pruitt and Mr. Hollister were talking animatedly to Walter Langdon. Close to the fire the Pomeroys, man and wife, conferred in low voices while the servants hovered on the outskirts, silent in the shadows.

"This is awful," I said inadequately, conventionally.

"I should hope to hell it is," said Ellen, guzzling Scotch like a baby at its mother's breast. "It's going to tie us all in knots for the next few months."

This was cold-blooded but I saw her point and, after all, it was her honesty which has always appealed to me. She had obviously not liked her father and I was oddly pleased that she had not, despite the crisis, acted out of character. It would have been such a temptation to weep and carry on. "What a funny way to kill someone," I said, not knowing quite what to say.

"Dynamite in the fireplace!" Ellen shook her head; then she put her drink down and looked at me. "It's the most impossible thing I've ever heard of."

"How do you feel?" I asked, suddenly solicitous.

"Numb," she said softly, shaking her head. "Did you ever find yourself not knowing what to think? Well, that's

27

the way I am now. I keep waiting for an alarm or something to go off inside me and show me how to act, what to feel."

"Your mother's taking it pretty well," I said.

"She's numb, too."

"Where were you when it happened?"

Ellen chuckled; for a moment she was like her old self "That would be telling!"

"With that boy?" I motioned to Langdon who was still talking to the politicos.

Ellen nodded, with a wicked smile. "We were just talking, in *his* room. He wanted to hear some stories . . . you know, life with father kind of things. . . ."

"I can imagine what you told him."

"Well, we really hardly had time. He had just told me he was being divorced from his wife, a Bennington girl, when the lights went out and . . ." She stopped abruptly, took a long drink; then: "Did you ever know any girls from Bennington? They're so terribly earnest. They *know* everything. I pity a boy like that being married to one of them."

"I suppose your compassion will very soon take a more positive turn," I said pompously: it was unseemly, I felt, to be talking about Ellen's sex life when her father, at this moment, lay dead in his study, guarded by the police, a blanket hung over the doorway to keep the cold air out of the rest of the house: part of one wall had been blown off while the furniture and the door, as well as the Senator, had all been shattered in the explosion.

"Oh, who cares," she said, without much interest. "How long do you think they'll take to figure all this out?"

"Who? The police? I haven't any idea."

"Well, I hope they're quick about it. It shouldn't take

long, God knows."

"You sound as though you know who killed him?"

The blue eyes flickered almost humorously in the waver-candlelight. "Of course I know, darling . . . but, for one reason and another, I'm not opening my mouth . . . wouldn't interfere for the world."

I felt very cold then . . . as though a blast of December air from that ruined study had penetrated the drawing-room and chilled me to the bone.

TWO

I

I was interviewed at four-twenty-seven in the morning by the Police Lieutenant who seemed nearly as weary as the rest of us.

"Full name," he mumbled mechanically. A plain clothes man took down my testimony. The three of us sat at one end of the dining-room table by the light of two candelabras: the candles were half-burned away.

"Peter Cutler Sargeant II."

"Age?"

"Twenty-nine."

"Occupation?"

"Public relations."

"By whom employed."

"Myself."

"Residence?"

"120 Christopher Street, New York City."

"How long have you known Senator Rhodes?"

"About one day."

"How did you happen to know him?"

"I was hired to handle his publicity. I only got here to-day . . . yesterday morning."

"What time did you come to the house?"

"About four-thirty in the afternoon."

"Did you go to the study at any time?"

"Not until after dinner, when the Senator asked me to join him there."

The Lieutenant opened his eyes and looked interested.

His voice lost its official mechanical tone. "What time did you leave?"

"Around one-thirty, I guess . . . just before he was killed."

"Where were you when he was killed?"

"I went back downstairs . . . for a drink. I ran into Miss Pruitt and we talked for a bit . . . she had left her cigarettes or something in the living-room . . . then I went upstairs. I was on the first landing when it happened; I was talking to Mr. Hollister."

"About what?"

"About what? oh . . . well, I don't remember. I think I'd just met him when it happened. We were both knocked down, and the lights went out."

"How did the Senator seem when you were with him?"

"I'm afraid I didn't know him well enough to say . . . I mean I don't know what he was like ordinarily. I got the impression that he was worried about something. I presumed it had to do with his announcement on Friday."

"At the Margarine Council.

I nodded. The Lieutenant lit a cigarette. What a wonderful break it was for him, I thought. This was going to be one of the most publicised cases in years. As a matter of fact, I was already trying to figure out some angle on how I might be able to cash in on it since my big job had been, to employ an apt phrase, blown to bits at the same time as my client. I was aware that I could get quite a price from my old newspaper the *New York Globe* if I could do a series of pieces on the murder, the inside story. I should have to cultivate the police, though.

"The Senator had many enemies," I volunteered.

"How do you know?" The Lieutenant was properly sceptical. "I thought you only met him yesterday."

"That's true but from what he told me just before he

31

was murdered, I should say that almost any one of a million people might have killed him."

"Why?"

"He was going to run for President."

"So?"

"He was being backed by some very shady characters."

"Names and addresses," the Lieutenant was obviously missing the point.

"I'm afraid it's not that simple," I said coolly. "I don't want to tangle with them and I don't expect you do either. Besides, I'm sure they didn't have anything to do with this murder . . . directly at least. The point is that *their* enemies might have wanted to do away with the Senator for the good of the country."

"I don't follow you. If we don't know who they are then how are we going to know who *their* enemies are, the ones who might want to kill Senator Rhodes?" The Lieutenant was not taking me very seriously, I decided, and I took this as a tribute to the stability of our country . . . the whole idea of a political murder, an assassination on ideological grounds, seemed like complete nonsense to him. The Presidents who had been killed in the past were all victims of crackpots, not of political plots. I decided to hold back my theories on political murder until I had a contract from the *Globe* safely in my pocket. In the meantime I had to be plausible.

"Let's put it this way," I said, speaking earnestly, as glibly as possible. " A lot of people didn't like the idea of a man like Rhodes becoming President. One of them, a crackpot maybe, might have got an idea that the best way to handle the situation would be to kill the Senator before the convention. For instance, right now, in this house, I should say there are four out-and-out political enemies of the Senator."

32

This had some effect. The Lieutenant stifled a yawn and sat up very straight. "Who are they?"

"Langdon, the newspaper-man . . . he's a young fellow, very liberal, he was sent here to write an attack on Rhodes for the *Advanceguard Magazine*. He couldn't have been more anti-Rhodes; and if he'd found out half as much as I did this evening he might have, for patriotic reasons, eased the Senator across the shining river."

"Across where?"

"Killed him. Then Miss Pruitt, though she's an old friend, was opposed to his running for President. Pomeroy, I gather, was a political enemy of Rhodes back in Talisman City and finally, after my little talk with Rhodes this morning, I was tempted to do him in myself."

"That's all very interesting," said the Lieutenant mildly. "But since you refuse to tell us who the Senator's supporters were, I'm afraid you aren't much help to this investigation. Please don't leave the house until further notice." And I was dismissed.

In the drawing-room I found Walter Langdon and the servants. All the others had been interviewed and had gone to bed. He looked haggered and pale and I felt a little guilty as I said good night, recalling the dark hints I had made to the Lieutenant . . . but they had been necessary. I was sure of that. This was not an ordinary murder . . . presuming that any murder could be called ordinary. I was both excited and frightened by the possibilities. Just as I got to the first landing, the lights came on again and, thinking of Rufus Hollister, I went to my room.

I was called for lunch at noon by the butler, who volunteered the information that no one had got up for breakfast except Mrs. Rhodes, who was now making arrangements for the Senator's burial at Arlington. I was also informed that the police were still in the house and that the street was crowded with newspaper-men and sightseers.

Ellen greeted me cheerily in the drawing-room. Wan winter sunlight shone in the room. All the ladies except Miss Pruitt, brave in rose, wore black. Everyone looked grim.

"Come join the wake," said Ellen in a low voice, pulling me over to one of the french windows.

"Has anything happened?" I asked, looking about the room for Mrs. Rhodes. She had not returned.

"Among other things, this," and Ellen gestured at the crowd of newspaper-men in the street below. Several police stood guard.

"Where is your mother?" I asked, as we stepped back out of the window; I had caught the glimpse of a camera being trained on us.

"She's still with the undertaker, I think. She should, be here for lunch. There's to be a service tomorrow morning at the Cathedral; then to Arlington." She was excited, I could see . . . I looked for some trace of sorrow in her face, but there was none: only excitement, and perhaps unease . . . a lot of skeletons were going to be rattled in several closets before this case was done. I picked up a newspaper and read on the front page how, "Statesman Meets Violent End", complete with a photograph of the late politico and an inset of the house with a gaping hole in it where the library had been. "I had no idea it made such a hole," I said, handing Ellen the paper. She put it back on the table: everyone had read it, I gathered.

"Nobody's been allowed to go in the study yet . . . not even Mother or me. Rufus is raising hell because he says there are important papers there."

Exactly on cue Rufus appeared in the doorway, his owl face peevish and his tweed suit looking as though he'd slept in it. He went straight to Ellen. "Have you any idea when your mother will be back?"

"I thought she'd be here by lunch-time. She said she would be finished in a few hours with the people at the Cathedral."

"We must do something about the files," said Rufus, looking at me nervously, as though unwilling to be more explicit.

"Files?" said the statesman's daughter; in political matters she was even more at sea than usual. Only one or two things really interested her . . . affairs of State left her cool and confused.

"Yes, yes," said Rufus impatiently. "All your father's supporters are listed in the secret files . . . along with their contributions: not that there is anything illegal going on," he chuckled weakly, "but if those names fell into the hands of our political enemies. . . ." He moaned softly; then the doors to the dining-room were thrown open and we went in to lunch.

I was surprised, as we took our seats, to find that Lieutenant Withers was also at the table. Needless to say, his presence threw something of a pall over what was, to begin with, a very gloomy group. The Lieutenant seemed calm, however, and I wondered whether or not it was usual for a police officer to dine with suspects. The fact that he was sitting next to Ellen I had duly noted and registered: he was no fool. She was susceptible and she was indiscreet. If he managed everything properly, he would know all he needed to know about the house of Rhodes in a few hours, pleasant hours.

"I can hardly believe this terrible thing has happened," said a rather nasal voice in my ear. I turned and saw for the first time that Mrs. Pomeroy was seated on my left. Her eyes were red and puffy and, from the sound of her voice, she had either been weeping or else she was catching a bad cold. As it turned out, she had a touch of the grippe.

"Our room was next to the Senator's study," she said, sniffing dolefully, her red eyes turned on me for sympathy. "Well, after this *terrible* thing went off the whole second floor was *freezing* cold, especially our room. I had had a slight cold when we left Talisman City . . . well, after last night's *terrible* event I *now* have the grippe. My temperature just before lunch was a hundred point three."

I suggested that she drink lemon juice in a glass of hot water and go to bed until the fever was over, but she wasn't much interested in my homely remedies. "It has been," she said in a low voice, "a *shattering* experience."

Especially for the Senator, I wanted to add, but decided not to. Across the table Ellen was deep in conversation with Lieutenant Winters. Walter Langdon, her next fiancé (or so I had thought), seemed forgotten; he was talking to Verbena Pruitt.

"You must have been very fond of Senator Rhodes," I said.

Mrs. Pomeroy nodded. "Oh, there were some *little* frictions between him and my husband . . . you know how men are, so *touchy,* concerned with trifles . . . but my own friendship with the Senator was, well, very real . . . and for many, *many* years." Something in her voice made me not only believe everything she was saying, but, more important, suggested a sudden, unexpected possibility. I looked at her curiously.

"How long had you known the Senator?" I asked gently.

"All my life," she said. "I was born in Talisman City, you know; Roger of course only moved there from Michigan about fifteen years ago."

"And you were married fifteen years ago?"

She giggled; then she sniffled and sneezed. I looked away until she had pulled herself together. "Not *quite* fifteen years ago," she said archly.

"You should do something about that cold."

"I'm taking pills . . . except for occasional political differences, our families have been very, *very* close all these years."

"What were those differences?"

"Oh, one thing and another. . . ." She gestured vaguely. "Political. My husband was for Roosevelt . . . that makes *quite* a difference, you know, out where we come from, that is. *I* was always for Dewey . . . so distinguished-looking, and so young. I think we need a young President, don't you?" I said that I hadn't given the question much thought. I was growing more and more suspicious, however; yet there seemed no way to find out what I wanted to know . . . unless Ellen knew, which was not likely. If Mrs. Pomeroy had been the Senator's mistress years ago, the fact would probably not have been well known by the Senator's family. I would have to find out, though. Mrs. Pomeroy, despite her red eyes and silly manner, was a very good-looking woman. If a man like Pomeroy should have a jealous nature. . . . An elaborate plot began to unwind in my head.

"Did you and Mr. Pomeroy visit here often?" I asked, the roast beef on my plate getting cold as I conducted my investigation.

She shook her head. "As a matter of fact we usually stay at the Mayflower and the Senator joins us for lunch over there."

"This is the first time you've stayed here in the house then?"

She nodded; for a moment her serene features seemed agitated, as though she suspected that I was questioning her for other than polite reasons. Quickly I began to gabble about sure-fire cures for head colds and the crisis passed.

We were given a little speech over the finger-bowls by Lieutenant Winters. He was as unlike a policeman as any man I've ever known, and he was obviously delighted with the whole business . . . no matter what happened, he was going to get a good deal of publicity; he was also going to meet a number of very important people who might do him some good one day. The murder of the Senator involved, in a sense, everyone in Washington political life, from the White House down to the most confused office-holder. He addressed us quietly, as though he were a fellow-guest, anxious to make a good impression.

"I may as well admit quite frankly, ladies and gentlemen, that we are baffled. We haven't the slightest idea who murdered Senator Rhodes." This unusual admission on the part of someone in authority made a considerable impression. I almost expected a polite round of applause . . . only the presence of death in the house prevented his audience from showing their pleasure at his originality.

"We are fairly confident that the murderer or murderers are, if you will pardon me, in the house at this time . . . but even of that we're not entirely sure. We *do* know that only someone who knew the Senator's habits fairly well could have contrived the . . . trap which worked so successfully. It would also seem that whoever did the murder could not have planned it too far in advance because the 5-X explosive was brought to the house only yesterday by Mr. Pomeroy. Four paper cartons of 5-X were kept in Mr. Pomeroy's room. Mr. Pomeroy discussed the new explosive with the Senator yesterday morning at the Senate Office Building in the presence of Mr. Hollister. He then joined Mrs. Pomeroy, Mr. Langdon, Miss Pruitt, Mrs. Rhodes and Miss Rhodes here in the house and there was, I am told, more talk of the new explosive. In short, all the guests, with the exception of Mr. Sargeant, knew about the 5-X, knew that Mr. Pomeroy had four cartons of it in his room, cartons which were to have been turned over to the army this afternoon with Senator Rhodes's recommendation. The cartons were kept in a special fireproof bag which was locked. Some time between four in the afternoon, when Mr. Pomeroy placed the bag in his cupboard, and one-thirty-six the next morning, when Senator Rhodes lit the fire in his study, the murderer went to Mr. Pomeroy's room, broke the lock on the bag and took out a single container which he then placed in the fireplace of the study. I believe that whoever did this must have known something about explosives because, had he taken all four and put them in the fireplace, the house would have been wrecked and the murderer killed along with everyone else." The Lieutenant paused. All eyes were upon him. The room was silent except for the rather heavy breathing of Mrs. Pomeroy beside me, struggling with her cold.

"Now," said the Lieutenant, with a juvenile actor's smile, "I realise that you people are very busy. Your affairs are very important to the country and the Department wants to do everything in its power to make this investigation as easy as possible for you. Unfortunately, until we have a clearer idea of what we're up against, you will have to be inconvenienced to the extent of remaining in this house for at least· a week." There was an indignant murmur; the official soft soap forgotten.

"Do you realise, young man," said Miss Pruitt, "that a national election is coming up? that I have a million things to do in the next few weeks?"

"I certainly do, Miss Pruitt. Everyone knows how important your work is, but we're all caught in the law. The Department, however, has agreed to allow you ladies and gentlemen to leave the house on urgent business, on condition that we always know where you are. Mrs. Rhodes has kindly consented to let us keep you here in the house for the next few days so that you'll be available for questioning. I realise how inconvenient this must be, but those are my orders." And the law took command. There were a few more complaints, but the comparative freedom allowed us put everyone in a better mood. The Lieutenant then permitted a recess until five o'clock, at which time there would be more questioning. Like children, we trooped out of the dining-room.

Verbena Pruitt was the first to leave, and, from the grim look on her face, I was quite sure that she would be in touch with the White House before many minutes had passed: after all, she was, in a sense, The American Woman. Mr. Pomeroy murmured something to his wife and also left. Walter Langdon went upstairs and Rufus Hollister tangled with the Lieutenant in my presence.

"Lieutenant, you must let me get certain papers out of the Senator's file. It's extremely urgent, as I've said before."

"I'm sorry, Mr. Hollister, but those papers are all being gone over by the Department. There's nothing I can do about it."

"I don't think you realise how serious this is, Lieutenant," said Hollister, flushing angrily. "The papers I want have nothing to do with the murder . . . I swear to you they don't. They involve, however, certain people of the greatest importance—the leaders of this country—and they were meant only for the Senator's eyes."

"We're not politicians," said the Lieutenant quietly . . . a little inaccurately, I thought. "We're not interested in the political implications of all this. Those papers are being gone over by men who are looking for only one thing: clues to the murder of Senator Rhodes. I don't need to tell you that they are discreet men. In any case, all the papers will be returned to your office in a day or two."

"You don't understand," said Rufus furiously, but there was very little he could say: the Lieutenant's attitude was perfectly reasonable, and legal. "I shall talk to the District Commissioners about this," he said finally; then he was gone. The Lieutenant sighed. I looked about me and saw that we were the only two left in the room. Ellen had quietly vanished . . . in pursuit of Walter Langdon, I presumed. The other policemen were all upstairs in the study. In the dining-room behind us the servants were cleaning up.

"You've got your work cut out for you," I said sympathetically.

He nodded. "It's like doing a tight-rope act. Do you realise the influence this gang has? I don't dare offend any of them."

"Or dare make a mistake."

"We don't make mistakes," said the Lieutenant, suddenly stuffy, a policeman after all, in spite of his college manners and Grecian profile.

"I might be able to help you," I said, going off on another tack: one which would interest him. He didn't react quite the way I would have liked, though.

"Why do you want to do that?" He was suspicious. It

41

gave me quite a turn to realise that this man regarded me as a possible murderer.

"Money," I said callously. Self-interest makes beasts of us all . . . and all men understand self-interest: it is the most plausible of motives, the one which is seldom ever questioned.

"What do you mean?"

"I mean that I would like very much to be the first to know who did the murder because I could then get quite a large sum of money from my old newspaper the *New York Globe* for an exclusive story on the murder."

"I thought you were in public relations."

"Before that I was assistant drama critic on the *Globe*. You may recall I was the one who did the story on the murder of Ella Sutton, the ballerina, last year. I made a good deal out of that particular story."

"I remember." I couldn't tell how he was reacting. Then: "Just how do you think you can help us?"

"Through the family," I said glibly. "Through Ellen Rhodes. You see, we used to be engaged. I can find out quickly a lot of things you people might never know."

"Such as?"

"What's really going on. What the Senator's true relationships were with this gang. By an odd coincidence almost everyone here disliked him, or had reason to."

"Except you?"

I was getting nowhere; I was also getting rather put out with this decorative arm of the law. "Except me. No, I didn't murder the old goat so that I could marry his daugther and get all his money. Having sat next to her at lunch, you are probably quite aware of Miss Rhodes's true nature."

Against his will, the Lieutenant grinned. I had made a chink in the official mask. I charged ahead. "We're old friends, that's all, Ellen and I. I have a hunch she knows a good deal about this, and I can find out what she knows, quickly."

"All just for a newspaper story?"

"Just!" I was genuinely outraged. "Yes," I said, more calmly, "just for a newspaper story, for the money and the publicity."

"We're not supposed to work with the Press . . . not like this, at this stage of an investigation."

"On the other hand, I'm not just the Press either."

"I'll say you're not. You're a murder suspect."

This was putting it too coldly, I thought. I shrugged and turned away. "In that case, you'll get no co-operation from me, Lieutenant. What I do know I'll keep to myself."

"What's the deal?" He was abrupt.

"I want to know what's going on. In exchange I'll find out things for you . . . family skeletons. On top of that, remember the pieces I'll do for the *Globe*'ll be widely reprinted and you, Lieutenant Winters, will be gettting a good deal of attention."

"What do you know?" I had won the first round.

"Pomeroy," I said. There was no need to explain further: we understood each other.

"Why Pomeroy?"

"Old enemy. The Senator was blackmailing him over that 5–X . . . at least, that's my guess. Rhodes wanted to be paid off either in cash or votes, probably the last. Pomeroy's a big gun in their state."

"How did you find this out?"

"I know a little about politics," I said quietly; as a matter of fact, I had figured out the whole plot at lunch. I didn't care to admit, at this point, however, that I was relying rather heavily on intuition and a few chance remarks dropped my way the day before by Rufus Hollister.

43

The Lieutenant extended to me his first confidence. "That's one way of looking at it," he said. "But the fact is the Senator refused yesterday to recommend Pomeroy to the Defence Department . . . Pomeroy admitted as much."

"I wonder, though, why the Senator's recommendation should be so important?" I asked, a little puzzled.

"Pomeroy was in bad with the Defence Department. They cancelled his contract last month."

I nodded as if I knew all this; actually it was a surprise; the first real lead. "I knew," I lied, "that he hoped his 5-X would put him back into business again."

"It's not very clear, though," said the Lieutenant sadly, moving over to the window which overlooked the street. Several newspaper-men were trying to get past the guards. Most of the crowd, however, had gone on about their business. "Why would Pomeroy want to kill the one man who could help him get his contract?"

"Isn't revenge one of the usual motives? along with greed and lust?"

"It's a little extreme . . . and obvious, too obvious." It was the first time that I had ever heard a member of any police department maintain that anything was too obvious: as a rule they jump wildly, and often safely, to the first solution that offers itself. This was a bright boy, I decided; I would have to handle myself very carefully around him.

"One other thing," I said, playing my only card.

"What's that?"

"Mrs. Pomeroy. I have an idea, a hunch."

"That what?"

"That she and the old boy were carrying on, a long time ago. It would complete the revenge motive, wouldn't it? Not only was Pomeroy angry about losing his contract, but he also had an old grudge against the Senator because of

44

something which had happened even before Pomeroy ever met his wife."

"Where'd you find all this out?"

"Deduction, I'm afraid. No evidence. At lunch today she made several remarks which started me thinking, that's all. I found out that she'd known the Senator all her life, that she was very fond of him . . . really so . . . that Pomeroy, as we know, was not; that Pomeroy came to the state only about fifteen years ago from Michigan and about the same time married the Senator's old friend, Mrs. P."

"It'll take a good deal of investigating to check on this."

"I know some short cuts."

"We could use them."

"You *do* think Pomeroy killed the Senator, don't you?"

The Lieutenant nodded: "I think he did."

3

After my session with Winters, I went upstairs and telephoned my office in New York. My secretary, a noble woman in middle life named Miss Flynn, admitted that she had been concerned about me. She gave me a quick report on the progress of my other clients: a hat company, three television actresses of the second rank, a comedian of the first rank, a society lady of mysterious origin but well-charted future, and a small but rich dog-food concern. All of my clients seemed reasonably pleased and the few problems which had arisen in my absence were settled over the phone with Miss Flynn. "I trust you will soon return to New York now that your client Senator Rhodes has been Gathered Up," said Miss Flynn ceremoniously.

"As soon as the police let us go," I said. "We're all in quite a spot."

"Washington!" said Miss Flynn with a note of disgust:

45

next to Hollywood she regarded it as the end, the absolute moral end of a country which was rapidly degenerating into something Roman and horrid.

After I had finished with Miss Flynn, I called my old editor at the *Globe,* and I managed to extort a considerable sum for a series of articles on the death of Senator Rhodes. I need not now recall the details of this transaction; enough to say that I did pretty well, considering the depressed state of the dollar.

My business over, I strolled downstairs to the second floor. At one end of the corridor, on the left, was the blanketed and guarded entrance to the study. Three bedrooms opened off that corridor. The one nearest the study was occupied by the Pomeroys. Across from it was Walter Langdon's and, next to his, was Rufus Hollister's room. To the right of the landing was another hall with four bedrooms opening off it. They were the rooms, I knew, of Senator Rhodes, of Mrs. Rhodes, of Ellen and Miss Pruitt. My room on the third floor was definitely in the outfield, up where the servants lived. On an impulse I went to Ellen's room and opened the door, without knocking.

Had I been half an hour later, I should probably have witnessed as fine a display of carnality as our Puritan country has to offer; happily, for my own modesty, I found Walter Langdon and Ellen still clothed, in spite of a steaming embrace on the bed which broke abruptly when they heard me. Langdon leaped to his feet like a track star warming up for the high hurdles; Ellen, an old hand at this sort of discovery, sat up more slowly and straightened her hair. "A pin just stabbed me in the back of the neck," she announced irritably, rubbing her neck. "Why the hell don't you knock?" Then, before I could answer, she turned to Langdon angrily and said: "I thought you said you locked the door?"

46

"I . . . I thought I did. I guess I turned the key over in the lock." He was blushing furiously and I could see that my ex-fiancée had aroused him. Embarrassed, he trotted into the bathroom and slammed the door behind him.

"A cooling-off period at this point in an affair is often considered very sound," I said smoothly. "It gives both parties an opportunity to determine whether or not their needs can be served only through sin."

"Oh, shut up! Where do you think you are? in a railway station? We were just talking, that's all . . . and now look what you've done."

"What have I done?"

"Embarrassed the poor little thing to death. It may take me days to get him back to where I had him before you came in."

"He's not that much of a baby," I said. "And your methods are foolproof, anyway."

"Hell!" said Ellen, in a mood of complete disgust and dejection.

"Anyway, I want to talk to you."

"What about?"

Before I could answer, Langdon came back into the bedroom noticeably soothed. "I'll see you later," he said calmly, and left the room.

"*Now* look what you've done!"

"You can finish your dirty work tonight," I said. "I want to talk to you about the murder."

"Well, what about it?" She was still angry. She went over to her dressing-table and sat down, repairing her blurred make-up. I ambled about the room, looking at the bookcase full of girls' stories and passionate adult novels, at the rather unfeminine décor.

"Was this always your room?"

She nodded. "Up until I got married it was."

47

"Where did you go after the marriage was annulled?"

"To a finishing school in New York. When I was thrown out of that, I stayed in New York. . . ."

"On a liberal allowance."

"Depends on your idea of liberal; now what about the murder?"

"They think, the police think, Pomeroy did it?"

"So?"

"Did he?"

"How should I know? Why don't you ask him?"

"I thought you said you knew who did it."

She laughed. "Did I say that? I must've been lit . . . or maybe *you* were lit . . . which reminds me, will you push that bell over there. It's getting near tea-time and I'm developing that funny parched feeling." I pushed the mother-of-pearl button.

"Who do you think did it?"

"My darling Peter, I'm not sure that even if I did know I would tell you. I realise that's an unnatural way to feel about the murderer of your own father, but I'm not a very natural girl, as you well know . . . or maybe *too* natural, which is about the same thing. If somebody disliked Father enough to kill him, I'm not at all sure that I would interfere. I have no feeling at all about him, about my father I mean. I never forgave him for that annulment . . . not that I was so much in love, though I thought I was, being young and silly, but rather because he had tried to interfere with me, and that's one thing I can't stand. Anyway, he was not very lovable, as you probably gathered, and when I could get away from home I did. I still don't know what on earth prompted me to come down here with you. I guess I was awfully high at Cambridge and it seemed like a fun idea. I regretted the whole thing the second I woke up on that train, but it was too late to go back." The butler interrupted the first serious talk I had ever had with Ellen, and, by the time half a Scotch mist had given her strength to face the afternoon, she was herself again and our serious moment was over.

"What do you know about the Pomeroys?" I asked when the butler had disappeared.

"What everybody knows. They're not that mysterious. He came to Talisman City in the late thirties and set up a factory . . . I suppose he had some capital to start with . . . he manufactured explosives. When the war came along he made a lot of money and the factory grew very big and he grew with it, got to be quite a power politically Then the war ended, business fell off and he lost his contract with the government, or so I was told yesterday."

"By whom?"

"By my father." She paused thoughtfully; then she swallowed the rest of the Scotch.

"Did he . . . did your father seem nervous to you?"

"You know, Peter, you're beginning to sound like that police Lieutenant . . . only not as pretty."

"I've got a job to do," I said, and I explained to her about the *Globe,* told her that she had to help me, that I needed someone who could give me the necessary facts about the people involved.

"You're an awfully fast operator," she said.

"That makes two of us."

She laughed; then she sat down beside me on the couch. "I'm afraid I've been away too long to be much help . . . besides, you know what I think or rather what I *don't* think about politics."

"I have a hunch that the murder doesn't have anything to do with politics."

"Your guess is as good as anybody's," said Ellen, and she helped herself to another drink.

49

"What about Mrs. Pomeroy?"

"What about her?"

"What's her relationship to your family . . . I gather she knew the Senator before she married Pomeroy."

"That's right. I remember her as a child . . . when *I* was a child, that is. She's about twenty years older than I am, though I'm sure she'd never admit that, even to her plastic surgeon."

"Plastic surgeon?"

"Yes, darling; she's had her face lifted . . . don't you know about those things? There are two little scars near her ears, under the hair. . . ."

"How was I supposed to see those?"

"*I* noticed them; I know all about those things. But that's beside the point. She's been around ever since I can remember. Her family were very close to ours . . . used to live right down the street, as a matter of fact: she was always coming over for dinner and things like that . . . usually alone. Her father was an undertaker and not very agreeable. Her mother didn't get on very well with my mother, so we seldom saw much of her. . . ."

"Just the daughter?"

"Yes, just Camilla. She was always organising the Young People's Voter Association for Father, things like that. She used to be quite a bug on politics, until she married Roger. After that we saw less of her . . . I suppose because Roger didn't get on with Father."

"I've got a theory that Mrs. Pomeroy and the Senator were having an affair."

Ellen looked quite startled; then she laughed. "Well, I'll be damned," she said. "Now that *is* an idea."

"Well, what's wrong with it?" I don't like my intuitions to be discredited so scornfully.

"Well, I don't know . . . it just seems terribly unlikely.

Father was never interested in women . . . as far as I know. *She* might have had a crush on him: that often happened when he was younger. There was always some dedicated young woman around the house doing odd jobs, but I'm sure nothing ever happened. Mother always kept a sharp eye on Father."

"I still think something might have happened."

"Well, what if it did?"

"It would give Pomeroy another reason for wanting to kill your father."

"So, after fifteen years, he decides to be a jealous husband because of something which happened before he met Camilla? Not very likely, darling. Besides, he had just about all the motive he needed without dragging that sheep in. You know, Peter, I think you're probably very romantic at heart: you think love is at the root of everything."

"Go shove it," I said, lapsing into military talk; I was very put out with her . . . also with myself: the Pomeroy business didn't make sense . . . it almost did, but not quite. There was something a little off. The motive was there, but the situation itself was all wrong. You just don't kill a man in his own house with your own weapon right after having a perfectly open quarrel with him over business matters. I was sure that Mrs. Pomeroy was involved, but, for the life of me, I couldn't fit her in. I began, rather reluctantly, to consider other possibilities, other suspects.

"But I love it," said Ellen cosily. "It shows the side of you I like the best." And we tusseled for a few minutes; then, recalling that in the next few hours I would have to have some sort of a story for the *Globe,* I disentangled myself and left Ellen to her Scotch.

As I walked down the hall, the door to Langdon's room

opened and he motioned for me to come in. The presence
of the plain-clothes man at the other end of the hall, guard-
ing the study, made me nervous: he could see everything
that happened on the second floor.

Langdon's room was like my own, only larger, American
maple and chintz, that sort of thing. On the desk his typewriter was open, and crumpled pieces of paper littered the
floor about it: he had been composing, not too successfully.

"Say, I hope I didn't bother you . . . my being in Miss
Rhodes's room like that." He was very nervous.

"Bother me?" I laughed. "Why should it?"

"Well, your being engaged to her and all that."

"I'm no more engaged to her than you are. She's engaged
to the whole male sex."

"Oh." He looked surprised; I decided he wasn't a very
worldly young man . . . I knew the type: serious, earnest,
idealistic . . . the sort who have wonderful memories and
who pass college examinations with great ease.

"No, I should probably apologise to you for barging in
like that, just as you were getting along so nicely." He
blushed. I pointed to the typewriter, to change the subject.
"Are you writing your piece?"

"Well, yes and no," he sighed. "I called New York this
morning and asked them what they wanted me to do now:
they sounded awfully indefinite, I mean, we never write
about murders . . . that's hardly our line. On the other
hand, there is probably some political significance in this,
maybe a great deal, and it would be quite a break for me
if I could do something about it . . . a Huey Long kind
of thing."

"I used to work on the *Globe*," I said helpfully. "But of
course we handled crime differently. You're right, I suspect,
about the political angle, but it won't be easy to track
down."

"I'm sure of it," said Langdon, with sudden vehemence. "He was a dangerous man."

"How long did it take you to figure that out?"

"One day, exactly. I've been here four days now . . . in that time I've found out things which, if you'd told me about them, I would never have believed possible, in this country, anyway."

"Such as?"

"Did you see the names of some of those people supporting Rhodes for President? Every Fascist in the country was on that list . . . every witch-hunter in public was backing his candidacy."

"You must have suspected all that when you came down here."

Langdon sat down on the bed and lit a cigarette; I sat opposite him, at his desk. "Well, naturally, we were on to him in a way. He was a buffoon . . . you know what I mean: an old-fashioned, narrow-minded demagogue always talking about Americanism. . . . Now our speciality is doing satirical articles about reactionaries . . . the sort of piece that isn't openly hostile, that allows the subject to hang himself in his own words. You have no idea how easy it is. Those people are usually well protected, by secretaries . . . even by the Press . . . people who straighten their grammar and their facts, make them seem more rational than they really are. So what I do is take down a verbatim account of some great man's conversation, selected of course, and publish it with all the bad grammar, and so on. I thought that's what I'd be doing here, but I soon found that Rhodes wasn't really a windbag, after all. He was a clever man and hard to trap."

"Then you found out all about his candidacy?"

"It wasn't hard."

"Where did you see those names? the names of the

supporters?" The memory of the indignant Rufus Hollister brow-beating Lieutenant Winters was still fresh in my memory.

Langdon looked embarrassed. "I . . . happened to find them, see them, I mean . . . in the Senator's study."

"When he wasn't there?"

"You make it sound dishonest. No, he asked me to meet him there day before yesterday; I got there before he did and I, well . . ."

"Looked around."

"I was pretty shocked."

"It's all over now."

He mashed his cigarette out nervously. "Yes, and I might as well admit that I'm glad. He could never have been elected in a straight election, but you can never tell what might happen in a crisis."

"You think that gang might have invented a crisis and tried to take over the country?"

He nodded, looking me straight in the eye. "That's just what I mean. I know it sounds very strange and all that, like a South American republic, but it *could* happen here . . ."

"As Sinclair Lewis once said." I glanced at the sheet of paper in the typewriter. A single sentence had been written across the top: *"And therefore think him as a serpent's egg Which hatch'd, would as his kind grow mischievous, And kill him in the shell."* Langdon was suddenly embarrassed, aware that I was reading what he had written. "Don't look at that!" He came over quickly, pulled the sheet of paper out of the typewriter. "I was just fooling around," he said, crumpling the sheet into a tight ball and tossing it into the waste-basket.

"A quotation?" I asked.

He nodded and changed the subject. "Do you think Pomeroy did it?"

"Killed Rhodes? I suppose so. Yet if he was going to kill the Senator, why would he have used his own 5-X, throwing suspicion on himself immediately?"

"Anybody could have got at the 5-X."

"Yes, but . . ." A new idea occurred to me. "Only Pomeroy knew how powerful one of those cartons of dynamite would be. Anybody else would be afraid of using something like that, if only because they might get blown up along with the Senator."

Langdon frowned. "It's a good point, but . . ."

"But what?"

"But I'm not so sure that Pomeroy didn't explain to us that afternoon about the 5-X, about the cartons."

I groaned. "Are you sure he did?"

"No, not entirely . . . I *think* he did, though."

"Yet isn't *that* peculiar?" I was off on another track. "Just why should he want to talk about his stuff in such detail?"

We talked for nearly an hour about the murder, about Ellen, about politics. . . . I found Langdon to be agreeable but elusive; there was something which I didn't quite understand . . . he suggested an iceberg: he concealed more than he revealed, and he was a very cool number besides. At last, when I had set his mind at ease about Ellen, I left him and went downstairs.

In the living-room I found Ellen and Mrs. Rhodes, pale but calm; they were talking to a mountainous, craggy man who was, it turned out, Johnson Ledbetter, the Governor of Senator Rhodes's home state.

"I flew here as quick as possible, Miss Grace," he said, with Mid-Western warmth, taking Mrs. Rhodes's hands in his, a look of dog-like devotion in his eyes.

55

"Lee would have appreciated it," said Mrs. Rhodes, equal to the occasion. "You'll say a few words at the funeral tomorrow?"

"Indeed I will, Miss Grace. This has shocked me more than I can say. The flag on the State Capitol back home is at half-mast," he added.

As the others wandered into the room, Ellen got me aside; she was excited and her face glowed. "They're going to read the will tomorrow, after the funeral."

"Looks like you're going to be a rich girl," I said, drying my sleeve with a handkerchief . . . in her excitement she had slopped some of her Scotch Mist on me. "I wonder if the police have taken a look at it yet."

She looked puzzled. "Why should they?"

"Well, darling, there's a theory going around that people occasionally get removed from this vale of tears by over-anxious heirs."

"Don't be silly. Anyway, tomorrow is the big day. That's why the Governor's here."

"To read the will?"

"Yes, he's the family lawyer. Father made him Governor a couple of years ago. I forget just why . . . you know how politicians are."

"I'm beginning to find out. By the way, have you got into that Langdon boy yet?"

"What an ugly question!" she beamed; then she shook her head. "I haven't had time. Last night would have been unseemly . . . I mean after the murder. This afternoon I was interrupted."

"I think he's much too innocent for the likes of you."

"Stop it . . . you don't know about these things. He's rather tense, I'll admit, but they're much the best fun . . . the tense ones."

"What a bore *I* must've been."

56

"As a matter of fact, you were; now that you mention it."
She chuckled; then she paused, looking at someone who
had just come in. I looked over my shoulder and saw the
Pomeroys in the doorway. He looked pale and weary; she,
on the other hand, was quite lovely, her attack of grippe
under control. The Governor greeted them cordially. Ellen
left me for Walter Langdon. I joined the Governor's group
by the fireplace. For a while I just listened.

"Camilla, you grow younger every year!" intoned the
Governor.

Mrs. Pomeroy gestured coquettishly. "You just want my
vote, Johnson."

"How long are you going to be with us, Governor?"
asked Pomeroy. If he was alarmed by the mess he was in,
he didn't show it; except for his pallor, he seemed much as
ever.

Mrs. Rhodes excused herself and went into the dining-
room. The Governor remarked that he would stay in town
through the funeral and the reading of the will; that he
was flying back to Talisman City immediately afterwards:
"Got that damned legislature on my hands," he boomed.
"Don't know what they'll do next." He looked about him
to make sure that no members of the deceased's family were
near-by; then he asked: "How did your session with the
Defence Department go?"

Pomeroy shrugged. "I was at the Pentagon most of the
day . . . I'm afraid the only thing they wanted to talk about
was the . . . accident."

"A tragical happening, tragical," declared the Governor,
shaking his head like some vast moth-eaten buffalo.

Pomeroy sighed: "It doesn't do my product much good,"
he said. "Not of course that I'm not very sad about this,
for Mrs. Rhodes's sake, but after all, I've got a factory back
home which has got to get some business or else."

57

"How well I know, Roger," said the Governor, with a bit more emphasis than the situation seemed to call for. I wondered if there was any business connection between the two. "We don't want to swell the ranks of the unemployed, do we?"

"Especially not if *I* happen to be one of the unemployed," said Roger Pomeroy dryly.

"I always felt," said his wife, who had been standing close to the Governor, listening, "that Lee's attitude was terribly unreasonable. He should've done *everything* in his power to help us."

"What do you mean?" asked the Governor.

Pomeroy spoke first, quickly, before his wife could elaborate. "Lee didn't push the 5-X as vigorously as I thought he should, that's all . . . that was one of the reasons I came to Washington on this trip . . . poor Lee."

"Poor Lee," repeated Mrs. Pomeroy, with real sincerity.

"A great statesman has fallen," said the Governor, obviously rehearsing his funeral oration. "Like some great oak, he leaves an empty place against the sky in our hearts."

Overwhelmed by the majesty of this image, I missed Pomeroy's eulogy; the next remark I heard woke me up, though. "Have you seen the will yet?" asked Mrs. Pomeroy, blowing her nose emotionally.

The Governor nodded gravely. "Indeed I have, Camilla. I drew it up for Lee."

"I wonder . . ." she began, but then she was interrupted by the appearance of Lieutenant Winters who joined us at the fireplace, bowed to the Governor and then, politely but firmly, led Mr. Pomeroy into the dining-room. Interviews, I gathered, had been going on for some time. The Governor detached himself from Camilla Pomeroy and joined Miss Pruitt on the couch and, considering the 'tragical' nature of the occasion, both were quite boisterous, talking politics eagerly.

My own interview with the Lieutenant took place right after he had finished with Pomeroy. I sat down beside him in the dining-room; the table was brilliantly set for dinner, massive Georgian silver gleaming in the dim light. Through the pantry door I could hear the servants bustling about. The usual plain-clothes man was on hand, taking notes. He sat behind Winters.

It took me several minutes to work my way past the Lieutenant's official manner; when I finally did, I found him troubled. "It won't come out right," he said plaintively. "There just isn't any evidence of any kind."

"Outside of the explosive."

"Which doesn't mean a thing since anybody in this house, except possibly you, could have got to it."

"Then you don't think Pomeroy was responsible?"

Winters played with a fork thoughtfully. "Yes, I think he probably was, but there's no evidence. He had no motive . . . or rather he had no more motive than several others."

"Like who?"

A direct question was a mistake I could see; he shook his head: "Can't tell you."

"I'm beginning to find out anyway," I said. I made a guess: "Rufus Hollister," and I paused significantly.

"What do you know about him?" Winters was inscrutable; yet I had a feeling that I was on the right track.

"It seems awfully suspicious his wanting to get into the Senator's office. I have a feeling there's something in there he doesn't want you to find."

Winters stared at me a moment, a little absent-mindedly. "Obviously," he said at last. "I wish I knew, though, what it was." This was frank. "We're still reading documents and letters. It'll take us a week to get through everything."

"I have a hunch you'll find your evidence among those papers."

"I hope so."

"None of the press has been let in on this yet, have they?"

Winters shook his head. "Nothing beyond the original facts. But there's a lot of pressure being brought to bear on us, from all over." I was suddenly sorry for him: there were a good many disadvantages to being mixed up in a political murder in a city like Washington. "That Pruitt woman, for instance . . . she was in touch with the White House today, trying to get out of being investigated."

"Did it work?"

"Hell no! There are times when the law is sacred. This is one of them."

"What about the will?" I changed *that* subject.

"I haven't seen a copy of it yet. The Governor won't let us look at it until tomorrow . . . says he 'can't break faith with the dead'."

"You may find out something from that, from the will."

"I doubt it." The Lieutenant was gloomy. "Well, that's all for now," he said at last. "The minute you turn up anything let me know . . . try and find out as much as you can about the family from Miss Rhodes: it'd be a great help to us and might speed things up."

"I will," I said. "I've already got a couple of ideas about Hollister . . . but I'll tell you about them later."

"Good." We both stood up. "Be careful, by the way."

"Careful?"

He nodded grimly. "If the murderer should discover that you were on his tail we might have a double killing to investigate.'

"Thanks for the advice."

"Think nothing of it." On a rather airy note, I went

60

back to the company in the drawing-room. My mind was crowded with theories and suspicions . . . at that moment they all looked like potential murderers to me. Suddenly, just before I joined Ellen and Walter Langdon, I thought of that quotation I had found in his room, the one he had snatched away from me. I also remembered where it came from: my unconscious had been worrying it for several hours and now, out of the dim past, out of my prep school days, came the answer: William Shakespeare . . . the play: *Julius Cæsar* . . . the speaker: Brutus . . . the serpent in the egg: Cæsar. There was no doubt about it. Brutus murdered the tyrant Cæsar. It was like a problem in algebra: Senator Rhodes equals Julius Cæsar; X equals Brutus. X is the murderer. Was Walter Langdon X?

THREE

I

I WENT to bed early that night. At dinner I drank too much wine and, as always, I felt bloated and sleepy. Everyone was in rather a grim mood so I excused myself at ten o'clock and went off to bed. I would have no visitors, I decided: Ellen was at work again on young Langdon and I was quite sure that they would be together, finishing what I had interrupted that afternoon.

I awakened with a start. For a moment I thought there was someone in the room and by the dim light of a street lamp I was positive that a figure was standing near the window. My heart racing, a chill sweat starting out on my spine, I made a quick lunge for the lamp beside my bed; it fell to the floor. Positive that I was alone in the room with a murderer, I jumped out of bed and ran to the door and flicked on the overhead light.

The room was empty and the figure by the window turned out to be my clothes arranged over an arm-chair.

Feeling rather shaky, even a little bit unwell, I went into the bathroom and took some aspirin. I wondered if I had caught Camilla Pomeroy's grippe; I decided that the wine had made me sick and I thought longingly of soda water, my usual remedy for a hangover. It was too late to ring for the butler. According to my watch it was a little after one o'clock, getting near the hour of the Senator's death, I thought as I put on my dressing-gown, ready now to go downstairs in search of soda.

I remember thinking how dark the stairway seemed. There was one dim light burning on the third-floor landing and, from the bottom of the stair-well, there was a faint light. The second landing was completely dark, however. Barely able to see, I moved slowly down the stairs, my hand on the banister. I was creeping slowly across the second landing, fumbling in my pockets for matches which were not there, when I suddenly found myself flying though space.

I landed with a crash on the carpeted stairs, stumbling forward, unable to stop my momentum; and, finally bumped all the way downstairs like a comedian doing pratfalls, landing at the feet of Lieutenant Winters.

"What in Christ's name happened?" he asked, picking me up and helping me into the drawing-room where the lights were still on.

It took me several minutes to get myself straightened out. I had twisted my left leg badly and one shoulder felt as though it had been dislocated. He brought me a shot of brandy which I gulped; it made a difference . . . I was able to bring him and the room into focus, my aches and pains a little less overpowering.

"They should install elevators," I said weakly.

"What happened?"

"Someone shoved me."

"Did you see who it was?"

"No . . . too dark. The lights were out on the second landing."

"What were you doing up?"

"I wanted to get some soda . . . upset stomach." I stretched my arms carefully; my shoulder throbbed. Nothing was broken, though.

"I wonder . . . " Then the Lieutenant was gone in a flash, running up the stairs two at a time. I followed him as fast as possible. When I reached the second landing, I was almost bowled over again by a gust of ice-cold air from the end of the hall. Then the lights came on and I saw Winters standing in front of the wrecked study; he was bending over the unconscious figure of a plain-clothes man. The blanket which had been hung over the study door was gone. I shivered in the cold.

"Is he dead?" I asked.

Winters shook his head. "Help me get him downstairs." Together we carried the man down to the drawing-room and stretched him out on a couch. Then Winters went to the front door and called one of the guards in and told him to look after his fallen comrade, to bring him to. "Somebody hit him," said the Lieutenant, pointing to a dark red lump over one temple. The man stirred and groaned. The other plain-clothes man went for water while Winters and I went back upstairs again.

It was the first time I had been in the study since my interview with the Senator. The lights were still out of order in this room. Winters pulled out a small pocket flashlight and trained the white beam of light on the room. There was a gaping hole in the wall where the fireplace had been. All the ruined furniture had been pushed to the far end of the room away from the hole. The various filing cabinets were open, and empty.

"You mean to say somebody got in here and took all the papers just now?" I was amazed.

Winters grunted, flashing his light over the shelves of books, over the photographs which hung crazily on the walls. "*We* took them," he said. "They're all down at headquarters. I wonder if our prowler knew that."

"A wasted trip then," I said, stepping back into the warm corridor, out of the cold room. Winters joined me a moment later. "Nothing's been touched as far as I can tell," he said. "We'll have the fingerprint squad go over the place tomorrow . . . not that I expect they'll find anything," he sounded discouraged.

"Maybe the guard will know something," I suggested cheerfully.

But the guard remembered nothing. He rubbed his head sheepishly and said: "I was sitting in front of that blanket when all of a sudden the lights went out and then I stood up and the next thing I knew *I* went out."

"Where's the light switch?" asked Winters.

"At the head of the stairs," said the man unhappily. "Right by the door to Mr. Hollister's room, in the centre of the landing."

"How could somebody turn off those lights without your seeing them?"

"I . . . I was reading." He looked away miserably.

Winters was angry. "Your job was to watch that corridor, to make sure that nothing happened, to protect these people as well as to guard the study."

"Yes sir."

"What were you reading?" I asked, interested as always in the trivial detail.

"A comic book, sir." And this was the master race!

Winters ordered the other plains-clothes man upstairs to take prints of the light switch. Then we went upstairs again and the Lieutenant proceeded to wake up everyone in the house for questioning. It was another late night for all of us and the discomfited politicos complained long and loudly but it did no good . . . it also did the law no good as far as I could tell. No one had heard my fall downstairs or the clubbing of the policeman; everyone had been asleep; no one knew anything about anything, and, worst of all, as far as the police could tell, nothing had been taken from the study.

I shall draw a veil of silence over the Governor's funeral oration: suffice it to say it was heroically phrased. The occasion, however, was hectic.

It was the first time I had been out of the house since the murder. I had no business in Washington and since my main interest was the murder I had spent most of the time talking to the suspects, calling various newspaper people I knew to check certain facts. Consequently, it was something of a relief to get out of the house, even on such an errand.

We were herded into several limousines and driven down-town, through a miserably grey sleet, to the National Cathedral, a vast Gothic building only half completed. A crowd was waiting for us outside one of the side doors. Flash-bulbs went off as Mrs. Rhodes and Ellen, both in heavy black veils, made a dash through the sleet from their car to the chapel door.

We were led by a pair of ushers down into a stone-smelling crypt, massive and frightening: then along low-ceilinged corridor to the chapel, brilliant with candles and banked with flowers: the odour of lilies and tuberoses was stifling.

Several hundred people were already there . . . including the police, I noticed. I recognised a number of celebrated political faces: Senators, members of the House, two Cabinet officers and a sprinkling of high military brass. I wondered how many of them were there out of sympathy and how many out of morbid curiosity, to survey the murder suspects of whom I was one. I was very conscious of this, as I followed Mrs. Rhodes and the Governor down the aisle to the front row. When we sat down the service began.

It was very solemn. I sat between Mr. Hollister and Mrs. Pomeroy, both of whom seemed much affected. It wasn't until the service was nearly over that I was aware of a slight pressure against my left knee. I glanced out of the corner of my eye at Mrs. Pomeroy, but her head was bowed devoutly and her eyes were shut as though she was praying. I thought it must be my imagination. But then, imperceptibly, the pressure increased: there could be no doubt about it, I was getting the oldest of signals in a most unlikely place. I did nothing.

At the cemetery, the service was even quicker because of the sleet which had now turned to snow. There were no tourists: only our party and a few camera-men. I thought it remarkable the Senator's wife and daughter could behave so coolly . . . for some reason only Rufus Hollister seemed genuinely moved.

When the last bit of hard black earth had been thrown on to the expensive metal casket, we got into the limousines again and drove back across the Potomac River to Washington and Massachusetts Avenue. It was a very depressing day.

The drawing-room, however, was cheerful by contrast. The fire was burning brightly in the fireplace and tea had been prepared. Mrs. Rhodes, a model of serenity, poured. Everyone cheered up a good bit, glad to be out of the black December day.

Ellen had thrown off her veil; she looked fine in her basic black dress. "I loathe tea," she said to me in a low voice as we sat together on a Heppelwhite couch at the far end of the room, close to the windows. The others were buzzing about the room in a dignified manner.

"Good for the nerves," I said; as a matter of fact, tea was exactly what I wanted at the moment. "What's next on the agenda?"

"Reading the will, I suppose."

"Your mother seems to be holding up awfully well."

"She's pretty tough."

"Was she very fond of your father?"

Ellen chuckled. "Now that's a leading question . . . as far as I know, she was, but you never can tell. They used to be very close, but then I've been away such a long time that I've rather lost touch with what's been going on." Across the room the Governor was talking gravely to Mrs. Rhodes, who looked pale but controlled.

Then I told Ellen about Mrs. Pomeroy.

She laughed out loud; she stopped when she saw Verbena Pruitt looking at us with disapproval. "I didn't know Camilla had it in her," she said with admiration.

"I only hope you're not jealous," I teased her.

"Jealous? Of Camilla?" Ellen was amused. "I wish the poor dear luck. I hope she has a good time . . . you will give her one?"

"I haven't thought that far ahead," I said loftily, wondering myself what I should do about this situation. I wasn't much attracted; on the other hand, if her husband was the murderer I should, perhaps, devote a little time to her. "By the way," I asked, "how is the *affaire* Langdon coming?"

Ellen scowled. "It's not coming at all. Every time something is about to happen the lights go out or someone gets murdered. At this present rate it will be weeks before anything happens."

"Were you with him last night?"

She smiled slyly.

"I don't think it would be very easy: with that guard watching the corridor all the time."

"He looks the other way. Besides, our rooms are on the same side and at the other end of the landing. He can't tell whether I'm going into my room or the one next to it."

"I see you've figured it all out."

"Don't forget that where the guard sits used to be my father's study, and that once upon a time Father used to work in there with the door open, keeping an eye on the hall and me, especially when we had young men staying in the house."

"Jezebel!"

"There are times when I think I may be a little abnormal," said Ellen calmly. Then, at a signal from the Governor, she got up and followed him into the dining-room: the room of all work. In a few minutes only Verbena Pruitt, Langdon and Mr. Pomeroy were left in the room. The four of us sat cosily about the fire. Pomeroy mixed drinks. From the other room came the monotonous, indistinct sound of the Governor's voice.

"I hope they'll be finished with us soon," said the great lady of American politics, scratching the point where her girdle stopped and her own firm flowing flesh began. She was in black now, but her hat was trimmed with quantities of imitation cherries.

"So do I," said Langdon gloomily, cracking his knuckles. "I have to get back to New York. The magazine is bothering the life out of me."

"I should think they'd be delighted to have one of their people in this house," I said reasonably, remembering my own newspaper days. Mr. Pomeroy handed me a Scotch and soda.

"I guess they think they have the wrong person here," said Langdon truthfully.

'Nonsense, my boy. It's all in your head. You can do anything you want to," Miss Pruitt fired her wisdom over a jigger of straight rye.

"But remember, Verbena, a murder story without a murderer isn't the most interesting thing in the world," Mr.

Pomeroy said quietly, shocking the rest of us a little since we all believed, deep down, that he *was* the murderer. If he was aware of our suspicions, he didn't show it. He went right on talking about the murder, in a tired voice. "It's one of those odd cases where no one is really involved, as far as we know . . . on the surface. I gather from the papers that some people think that because of the weapon used and because of my own troubles with Lee I killed him . . . but, aside from the fact I *didn't* kill him, doesn't it seem illogical that I would use my own 5-X, immediately after a quarrel, to blow him up? It's possible, certainly, but too obvious, and I will tell you one thing: considering the people involved in this affair nothing, I repeat *nothing,* is going to be simple or obvious." There was an embarrassed silence after this.

"You *know* none of us think you did it," said Verbena Pruitt, with a good imitation of sincerity. "Personally, I think one of those servants did it . . . that butler. I never have approved of this habit of leaving money to servants, to people who work for you every day . . . it's too great a temptation for them."

I tried to recall who the butler was; I couldn't, only a vague blur, a thin man with a New England accent.

"I don't see why they think one of *us* had to do it," said Langdon petulantly. "Anybody could have got in this house that day and planted the stuff in the fireplace. According to the butler, two plumbers were on the second floor all that afternoon and nobody paid any attention to them."

This was something new. I wondered if Winters knew this. "Perhaps the plumbers didn't have any motive?" I suggested.

"Perhaps they weren't plumbers," said Pomeroy, even more interested than I in this bit of information.

"Hired assassins?" This was too much, I thought . . .

still it happened quite often in the underworld . . . and the political world of Lee Rhodes had, in more than one place, crossed the world of crime.

"Why not?" said Pomeroy.

"But the reason the police think someone on the inside did it was because only a person who knew the Senator's habits well could have figured out how to kill him that way, with the stuff in the fireplace." I was sure of this: for once the official view seemed to me to be right.

Langdon dissented, to my surprise. "You're going under the assumption that the only people in the world who knew the Senator's habits were in this house as guests that night. You forget that a good many other people knew him even better than most of us did . . . people who would have been just as capable of blowing him up . . ."

"Perhaps," I said, non-committally. I made a mental note to call Miss Flynn in New York and have her check up on the past of Walter Langdon. I didn't quite dig him, as the jazz people say.

Suddenly there was an unexpected sound from the dining-room . . . a little like a shriek, only not so loud or so uncontrolled: an exclamation . . . a woman's voice. Then the double doors were flung open and Mrs. Rhodes, white-faced, rushed through the room to the hall, not stopping to acknowledge our presence. She was followed by Ellen, also pale and odd-looking, and by Mrs. Pomeroy, who was in tears. Outside, the Governor and Rufus Hollister were deep in an argument while, behind them, several servants, minor beneficiaries, trooped back to the kitchen.

Mrs. Pomeroy, without speaking even to her husband, left the room close on the heels of Mrs. Rhodes. Pomeroy, startled, followed her.

It was Ellen who told me what had happened, told me

71

that Camilla Pomeroy, born Wentworth, was the illegitimate daughter of Leander Rhodes and a principal heir to his estate.

3

"Who would have thought it," was Ellen's attitude when we got away from the others after dinner; we pretended to play backgammon at the far end of the drawing-room. Everyone had been shocked by the revelation. Winters was having a field day and Mrs. Rhodes was hiding in her room.

"Rufus is trying to keep it out of the papers, but the Governor says that it's impossible, that under the circumstances the will would have to be made public because of the murder. It's going to kill Mother."

"Did you ever suspect anything like this?"

She shook her head. "Not in a hundred years. I knew Camilla adored Father, but I think I've already told you there was almost always some goose girl around making eyes at him and getting in Mother's hair."

"Did she know?"

"Mother? I don't think so. You never can tell, though. She's just about the most close-mouthed person in the world . . . has to be in politics. She *seemed* awfully shocked."

"I'm not surprised . . . it must have been awful for her, hearing it like that . . . in front of everyone."

Ellen grimaced. "Awful for everybody."

"I wonder why he'd admit something like that . . . even in his will."

"I suppose he never thought he'd die this soon . . . besides, it could have been kept quiet if there hadn't been a murder to complicate things."

"How much does she get?"

"A little over a million dollars," said Ellen, without batting an eye.

I whistled. "How much of the estate is that?"

"Around a third. Mother and I each get a third . . . and then the servants get a little and Rufus gets all the law books, and so on."

"This changes everything."

"I don't know."

"Do you still think you know who killed your father?"

She looked at me vaguely. "Darling, I haven't the faintest idea who you mean."

"You did a couple of days ago."

"Now I'm not so sure." She was obviously not listening to me. She kept rolling the dice on to the backgammon-board, again and again without looking at the numbers.

"What made you say you thought you knew?"

"I've forgotten." She seemed irritated. "Besides, why is it so important to you?"

"I have to do a story."

"Then write about something else."

"Don't be silly. Anyway, even if I didn't have to worry about the *New York Globe*, I'd be worried on my own account . . . being shut up like this with a murderer . . . in the same house."

"Oh, stop being so melodramatic! You haven't the faintest connection, as far as I can see, with all this . . . why should *you* be in danger?"

"Because of my theories," I said a little pompously . . . as a matter of fact, I was still completely at sea.

Ellen said a short four-letter word which communicated her opinion of my detective abilities with Saxon simplicity.

"Tell me, then," I said coolly, "why I should be shoved downstairs in the dark with such force that I could've broken my neck . . ."

"If your head hadn't been so solid," said the insensitive Ellen, rolling snake eyes. "By the way, did you get a look at whoever it was who pushed you?"

"How could I? I told you it was dark on the landing."

"I must say all that's very exciting . . . it's the one really interesting thing that's happened since the murder."

What a cold-blooded piece she was, I thought. She acted as though she were in a theatre watching a play, interested only in being shocked or amused. I wondered if *she* might not have been the illegitimate daughter after all . . . no Electra she, as *Time* Magazine would say. "It would be a lot more interesting if they could find out what the murderer wanted in that room."

"Why? Did he take anything?"

"Not as far as the police could tell. There weren't any papers there, anyway . . . everything had been taken down to headquarters."

"Poor Rufus."

"Why do you say that?"

"He's terrified all his political shenanigans will be found out . . . he and Father were awfully close, you know . . . I suspect they were involved in all sorts of deals which might not bear investigating."

"Well, if there was anything shady, the police haven't found it," I said, with more authority than I actually had: I was not naïve enough to think Lieutenant Winters had confided all he knew to me. "I wonder if Rufus could have been the one who knocked the guard out last night, and pushed me downstairs."

"I wouldn't be at all surprised."

"I doubt if there was anything in there the murderer could have wanted . . . if there had been he would have got it the night of the murder, *before* the murder . . . unless he left something by mistake."

"Which the police would have found by now."

There were so few real leads, I thought sadly. Pomeroy's fued over the 5-X; Langdon's strange quotation and highly political attitude . . . very much the fanatic type; Rufus Hollister's terror of certain documents falling into the hands of the police; Camilla Pomeroy's unexpected relationship to the Senator . . . her large inheritance which provided both her and her husband with ample motive for murder. But had they known she was included in the will? Had Pomeroy known that his wife was the Senator's daughter? This was a question which should be cleared up soon: it would make a great deal of difference.

Across the room I saw Langdon excuse himself and go upstairs; a moment later Ellen gave a vast stage yawn and said: "I'm worn out, darling. I think I'll go up now."

"And get a little shut-eye?" I mocked.

"Don't be a cad," she said grandly, and swept out of the room.

I found Winters in the dining-room going over what looked like a carbon copy of the will. He looked up when I came in; his ever-present plain-clothes man made a move to bar my way, but Winters wearily waved him aside. "Come on in."

I sat beside him at the table. I asked the important question first.

He nodded in answer. "Yes, Pomeroy knew who his wife's father was. It seems she told him last year . . . at the height of his quarrel with the Senator . . . she thought it would make him more reasonable."

"Did it?"

Winters sighed. "The big question."

"There's a bigger question . . . did either of them know about the will?"

"It'll be a long time before we figure that one out," said

75

the Lieutenant grimly. "Both deny having known anything about it. But . . ."

"But you think they did."

He nodded. "The Governor drew up the will . . . he's also Pomeroy's lawyer, and an old friend."

"Can't very well grill a Governor."

"Not directly."

Remembering the pressure on my knee at the Cathedral, I had an idea. "I think I can find out something about the will from Mrs. Pomeroy." I told him about the knee-pressing episode. He was interested.

"It would be a great help. It'd just about wind up the case we're making against Pomeroy: double motive, the weapon, the opportunity . . ."

"Two more suspects, though."

"Who?"

"Hollister . . . he and the Senator were obviously involved in some illegal activities. And Langdon, who's something of a fanatic." I related the business about the quotation, but it was much too tenuous for the official mind. As for Hollister, we both agreed that he was an unlikely murderer since, had he done away with the Senator, he would have taken care to have got all the incriminating papers out of the study first. With a promise to do my best with Mrs. Pomeroy, I left Winters to his bleak study of the will.

I was staring at my typewriter with a feeling of great frustration when there was a rap on my door. "Come in," I said.

Rufus Hollister put his head inside the door, tentatively, like one of those clowns at a carnival who makes targets of their heads for customers with bean-bags. "May I come in?"

"Sure." I motioned to the arm-chair opposite me. He sat down with a moan, crumpled, I should say. I sat very straight at my desk, the light behind my head, ready to yell if he pulled a gun on me.

But if Rufus was the murderer, he was not in a murdering mood. In fact, he was hardly coherent. "Just wandering by," he mumbled.

"If I had a drink I'd offer it to you."

"Quite all right. I've had a few already . . . maybe too many." He sighed again deeply; then he took off his thick spectacles and rubbed his owl eyes . . . they were rather tiny, I noticed . . . quite different without the magnifying glasses.

"Do the papers know yet?" I asked, recalling that I was, after all, in the public relations business.

"Know?" He blinked at me.

"About the will? About Mrs. Pomeroy?"

"Not yet. I suppose they will be told tomorrow."

"Has Mrs. Rhodes tried to do anything to keep the news out of the papers?"

"You know as well as I do there isn't any way of keeping something like that secret."

"I know. I just wondered if she had tried to keep it quiet."

Rufus shrugged. "I haven't seen her since the will was read." There was a long pause. I wondered when he would come to the point; he obviously had some reason for wanting to see me. But he said nothing. He stared blankly at the floor; he seemed a little drunk.

Growing nervous, I said: "Is there anything in particular you think I should do for the family . . . in the way of public relations?"

"What? Oh . . . oh, no. It's out of our hands now, I'm afraid." He put his glasses on again and looked at me; with an effort he pulled himself together. "You're doing a story about all this, aren't you?"

I nodded. "For the *Globe*."

"I wish you'd check with me before you send them anything."

"Certainly . . . if I can ever find out anything to write for them."

"You will," he said ominously. "Soon, very soon."

I waited for more, but he had drifted off again. "Tell me," I asked, "did the Pomeroys come here much in the old days?"

He shook his head. "Pomeroy himself seldom came to the house. Mrs. Pomeroy did . . . fairly often."

This was unexpected. "I seem to remember her telling me . . . or somebody telling me that they never came here, either of them."

"She was here often."

"And she knew the Senator's habits well?"

He nodded; he knew what I was getting at, but he refused to volunteer anything. He changed the subject. "You and Ellen are old friends, aren't you?"

I said that we were.

"She made her father unhappy, very unhappy," said Mr. Hollister, rubbing his palms together. It was my turn to wonder what *he* was getting at. "Her life has not been exemplary."

"You're not kidding!"

"At one time he even threatened to cut her off without a cent."

"You mean when she married?"

"Later . . . last year when she was making a scandal of herself in New York."

"I can't exactly blame him."

"Poor man . . . he had so many terrible things to bear during his life."

"Why didn't he cut her off?"

78

"Ah! You know her. She came down from New York last month and they had a terrible scene. I suppose she threatened to disgrace him once and for all if he didn't give her the money she needed . . ."

"That sounds like Ellen."

"What could he do? She was his own flesh and blood . . ."

"And he was about to run for President . . ."

"Exactly. She got her way . . . we always supposed that she had left for good until she came back with you this week. Why?"

"Why what?"

"Why did she come back?"

"I haven't the faintest idea. It seemed like a good idea, I suppose. We had both been drinking."

"*That* explains it then?"

"She drinks a lot," I added, but this wasn't necessary . . . and still Mr. Hollister hadn't come to the point.

"By the way," he asked suddenly, "did you have any idea who pushed you last night?"

I shook my head; then I had an idea . . . a daring one. "I didn't see who it was," I said; then I added, slowly, looking straight at him: "But I have a very good idea who it was."

I wasn't able to interpret his reaction; he turned pale, but I couldn't tell if it was from guilt or astonishment. "Did you see *anything?*" he asked.

"A glimpse, that was all. I couldn't say for sure who it was, but I have a good idea."

"Who . . . who do you think it was?" He sat on the edge of his chair, his breath coming in quick gasps.

"I can't tell you," I said, waiting for some sign . . . but there was none, other than this excitement.

"Be careful," he said at last. "Be careful what you say to the police. The repercussions might be serious."

"I know what I'm doing," I said quietly, never more confused.

"I hope so. By the way, did the Senator talk to you at all about family matters?"

"No, not much . . . a little about Ellen, since he thought I was going to marry her, but I straightened all that out."

"And the campaign . . . did he talk about that? About those close to him in it?"

"Not a word . . . just general talk."

"That was a pity," he said cryptically; then he rose to go. I stopped him momentarily with a direct question.

"Who killed him?" I asked.

"Pomeroy," said Rufus Hollister; then he said good night and left me.

4

I undressed slowly, thinking of what had been said. Hollister made me uneasy . . . I couldn't tell just why, but I had more than a faint suspicion that he might have been the murderer after all. It was evident that he had visited me to try and find out whether or not I had recognised whoever it was who'd shoved me down the stairs, and it was possible that he was the one who had done the shoving . . . the murder, too? It was perplexing. I locked the door, leaving the key in the lock. I was nervous.

Then, dressed in pyjamas, I sat down at the desk again and began to type idly. Pomeroy, Langdon, Hollister, Miss Pruitt, Mrs. Rhodes, Ellen, Mrs. Pomeroy. There was a knock on the door. I flipped on the overhead light (if I was to be shot, I preferred a great deal of light); then I unlocked the door and slowly opened it. To my surprise Camilla Pomeroy, wearing a pale blue silk négligée, stood in the doorway.

"May I come in?" she asked in a low voice.

Startled, I said: "Yes." I locked the door behind her. She stood in the centre of the room as though unsure of herself, not certain what to do next. "Sit down," I said, trying to be as casual as I could under the circumstances. Uncertainly, she went over to the arm-chair recently vacated by Rufus Hollister. She sat down; I sat opposite her. She was nearly as embarrassed as I.

"I . . . couldn't sleep," she said at last with a nervous laugh.

"Neither could I." We looked at one another stupidly. I noticed with surprise how lovely she was . . . noticed also that she had not yet been to bed: her make-up was perfect and her hair was carefully arranged.

"You must think it awful of me coming in here like this in the middle of the night." This came out in a rush.

"Why, no . . . not at all."

"I had to talk to someone." She *did* sound desperate, I thought. I wondered whether or not I should suggest that her husband might be the man to talk to at this time of night. She guessed what I was thinking, though. *"He's* asleep. He takes sleeping-pills . . . very strong ones, since . . . it happened." She almost sobbed. I wondered if I should get her a Kleenex. But she got a hold of herself. "Do turn that light out," she motioned to the bright one overhead. "A woman doesn't like too direct a light when she's been crying." Her attempt at frivolity was pretty ghastly, but I turned out the light. She looked even better in the warm glow of a single lamp . . . and of course her looking better hardly helped the cause.

"Thank you," she murmured. She pulled the négligée tight about her throat, emphasising the full curve of her breasts. I wondered if she intended this.

"I had to talk to someone," she repeated. I looked at her

brightly, like one of those doctors in an advertisement: ready to make some comment about halitosis or life insurance.

"About . . . everything," she said.

"About the will?"

"Yes." She looked at me gratefully; glad that I was coming around. "Tomorrow all the world will know," she said, with a certain insincere over-statement which made me think that for a million dollars she didn't give a damn *what* the world knew.

"There's nothing you can do about it now," I said soothingly.

"If only there were!" She still held one hand close to her throat, the way bad actresses do in moments of crisis on stage.

"People forget so quickly," I said.

"Not in Talisman City," she snapped. Then, recollecting herself, she added more softly: "The world is so unkind."

I allowed that, all things considered, this was so.

"It was unfair of Lee . . . of my father to act the way he did."

"You mean in . . . *being* your father?" I was dense.

"No, I mean in declaring to all the world my . . . shame."

To which I replied: "Ah."

"I can't think why he chose to do it like this, so publicly."

"Probably because there wasn't any other way of leaving you his money."

There was no real answer to this, so she exclaimed again how terrible it all was.

"What does your husband think about it?"

She sighed.

"Did he know all along that . . . about the Senator and you?"

"Oh yes. He's known for a year."

"And the will . . . did he know about that, too?"

She closed her eyes, as though in pain. "Yes," she said softly, "I think he knew about the will, too. I think the Governor told him."

"But they never told you?"

She hesitated. "No," she said. "Not exactly. I suppose I knew, in a way, but they never actually told me." This was a bit of news, I thought. The outline of a plot suggested itself to me. "My husband never liked to talk about it . . . neither did I. It was just one of those things. What was that?" She started, and looked towards the door.

Nervously, expecting an angry husband, I opened the door and looked out. The hall was empty. "It was the wind," I said, turning around. She was standing directly behind me . . . I could smell the musk and rose of her perfume.

"I'm frightened," she said, and this time she was not play-acting. I moved back into the room, expecting her to move too but she did not.

An hour passed.

I sat up and looked down at her white body sprawled upon the bed; the eyes shut and her breathing regular and deep. "It's late," I said in a low voice.

She smiled drowsily and opened her eyes. "I haven't been so relaxed in a long time," she said.

"Neither have I," I lied nervously; I didn't like the idea of being treated like some kind of sedative.

She sat up on one elbow and pushed her hair back out of her eyes. She was obviously proud of her body; she arranged it to look like the Duchess of Alba. 'What on earth would my husband say."

"I hope I never know," I said devoutly.

She smiled languorously. "He'll never know."

"Great thing sleeping-pills."

"I don't make a habit of this," she said sharply.

"I didn't say you did."

"I mean . . . well, I'm not promiscuous, that's all . . . not the way Ellen is."

I was a little irritated by this. Somehow, I felt she had no business talking about Ellen like that since, for all she knew, we might really have been engaged. "Ellen's not that bad," I said, pulling on my pyjamas. Then I handed her her négligée. "You don't want that cold to get worse, do you?"

Reluctantly she snaked into the blue silk. "I'm very, very fond of Ellen," she said, with a brilliant insincere smile. "But you have to admit she's a law unto herself."

I was about to make some crack about their being sisters under the skin when it occurred to me that this might be tactless since, as a matter of fact, they *were* sisters in a way.

She asked for a cigarette, and I gave her one. "Tell me," she said, exhaling blue smoke, "how long do you think it'll be before the police end this case?"

"I haven't any idea."

"But you *are* working with Lieutenant Winters, aren't you?"

This was shrewd. "How did you know?"

"It wasn't hard to guess. As a matter of fact, I caught the tail end of a telephone conversation you were having with some newspaper in New York." She said this calmly.

"An eavesdropper!"

She chuckled. "No, it wasn't on purpose, believe me; I was trying to call a lawyer I know in the District . . . you were on this extension, that's all."

"I haven't any idea," I said. "About the murder . . . about how long it'll be before the police make an arrest."

"I hope it's soon," she said, with sudden vehemence.

"So do all of us."

She was about to say something . . . then she stopped herself. Instead she asked me about the affair on the landing, and I told her that I had seen no one. She looked disappointed. "I suppose it was too dark."

I nodded. "Much too dark."

She stood up then and arranged her hair in a mirror. I stood beside her, pretending to comb my own hair. I was aware of her reflection in the glass, very pale, with the dark eyes large and strange, staring at me. I shuddered. I thought of those stories about vampires which I had read as a child.

She turned around suddenly; her face close to mine . . . her eyes glittering in the light. "You must help me," she said, and her voice was strained.

"Help?"

"He'll try to kill me . . . I'm sure of it. Just the way he killed my father."

"Who? Who killed your father? Who'll try to kill you?"

"My husband," she whispered. Then she was gone.

FOUR

I

BEFORE breakfast, I composed a communiqué for the readers of the *New York Globe;* then, just as the morning light began to stream lemon yellow across the room, I telephoned it to New York, consciencelessly allowing the Rhodes family to pay for it; I was aware that my conversation was being listened to by a plain-clothes man on an extension wire: I could hear his heavy breathing.

My story was hardly revelatory, but it would, I knew, keep me in business a while longer, and it would also give the readers of the *Globe* the only inside account of how the bereaved family was taking their loss: "Mrs. Rhodes, pale but calm, was supported by her beautiful daughter Ellen Rhodes yesterday at the National Cathedral while thousands. . . ." It was the sort of thing which some people can turn out by the yard, but which I find a little difficult to manage; a mastery of newspaper jargon is not easily come by: you have to have an instinct for the ready phrase, the familiar reference. But I managed to vibrate a little as I discussed, inaccurately, the behaviour of the suspects at the funeral.

I smiled as I hung up the phone and put my notes in the night table drawer; I had thought of a fine sentence: "While your correspondent was attending the funeral services for the late U.S. Senator Leander Rhodes at the Washington Cathedral yesterday morning, a knee belonging to the attractive Camilla Pomeroy of Talisman City, wife of

Roger Pomeroy, the munitions-maker, was pressed against your correspondent's knee . . ."

I lit a cigarette and thought idly of my session with Mrs. Pomeroy the night before. There had been a faint air of the preposterous about everything she'd said, if not done. The one thing she could do well was hardly preposterous: she was even better geared, as they say, than her half-sister . . . though Ellen would have been furious to know this. Ellen, like all ladies of love, thought there was something terribly special about her performances when, in fact, they were just about par. But I am not faintly interested in such things early in the morning, and despite the vividness of Camilla's production I was more concerned, at eight in the morning, with what she had said.

I have a theory that I think best shortly after I wake up in the morning. Since no very remarkable idea has ever come to me at *any* time, to prove or disprove my theory, I can happily believe that this is so, and my usual plodding seems almost inspired to me in these hours between waking and the clutter and confusion of lunch-time.

I had a lot to think about. Lying on the bed in my bath-robe, arms crossed on my chest like a monument, I meditated. Camilla Pomeroy is the daughter of Leander Rhodes. She has inherited a million dollars from her father, despite the bar sinister. She married a man who disliked Rhodes. Rhodes disliked *him* . . . why? (The first new question that had occurred to me; jealous of his daughter? Not likely. Why then did Rhodes dislike his son-in-law to such an extent he would queer his chances of staying in business? Today's problem.) And why did Pomeroy not like Rhodes? Political enemies . . . Senator unco-operative about business matters . . . a deal, somewhere? a deal which fell through? Someone crossed up someone else? A profitable line of inquiry.

And Camilla Pomeroy? What was she trying to do? There was no doubt that she genuinely believed her husband killed her father, but why then had she come to me instead of to the police? Well, that was easily answered. She knew that I was in touch with Winters. That I was writing about the case for the *Globe* . . . anything she planted with me would get to the attention of the police, not to mention the public, very quickly. But she had asked me to help her. How? Help her do what? Now, there was a puzzle. The thought that she might not like her husband, might in fact like to see him come to grief for the murder of her father, occurred to me forcibly. If she did not care for Pomeroy and *had* cared for her father; if she believed Pomeroy killed the Senator, then the plot became crystal clear. She could not testify against her husband, either legally or morally (socially, that is), but she could take care of him in another way. She could spill the beans to someone who would then spill them to the police, saving her the humiliation and danger of going to the police herself. That was it, I decided.

Of course she could have killed her father to get the money and then, in an excess of Renaissance high spirits, implicated her husband. But that was too much like grand opera. I preferred not to become enmeshed in any new theory. I was perfectly willing to follow the party line that Pomeroy did it. After all, what I had learned from Camilla corroborated what everyone suspected. Yet why had absolutely no evidence turned up to clinch the case?

I was the first down to breakfast. Even before the ill-starred house party the family evidently breakfasted when they felt like it, not depressing one another with their early morning faces.

I whistled cheerily as I entered the dining-room. Through the window I could just glimpse a plain-clothes man at the door. "An armed camp," I murmured to myself, in Bold Roman. The butler, hearing my whistled version of "Cry" complete with a special cadenza guaranteed to make even the heartiest stomach uneasy, took my order for breakfast, placed a newspaper in front of me and stated the hope, somewhat formally, that the morning would be good for one and all.

The murder was on page two, moving slowly backwards until a *Sudden Revelation* or *Murder Suspect Indicted* brought it back to its proper place between the Korean war and the steel strike. There was a blurred photograph of the widow and daughter in their weeds at the cemetery . . . also a few hints that an arrest would presently be made. As yet there was no mention of the will . . . that would be the plum for the afternoon papers, and my own *New York Globe* would have the fullest story of them all ("pale but unshaken Camilla Pomeroy heard the extraordinary news in the dining-room. . . ."). I was disagreeably struck, as I often am, with my elected rôle in life: official liar to our society. My life work is making people who are one thing seem like something very different . . . manufacturers are jailed for adulterating products, but Press agents make fortunes doing the same thing to public characters. Then, to add to all this infamy, I was now using for my own advantage a number of people I knew more or less well . . . all for a story for the *New York Globe,* for money, for publicity. *Mea Culpa!*

Fortunately what promised to be an orgy of guilt and self-loathing was cut short by the arrival of ham, eggs, coffee and Ellen, dashing in black.

"Oh, how good it smells! I could eat the whole hog," said that dainty girl, dropping into the chair opposite me. She looked as though she could, too, ruddy and well rested.

"Did you sleep well?" I asked maliciously.

"Don't be a pry," said Ellen, giving her order to the butler and grabbing the newspaper from me at the same time. I noticed with amusement that she only glanced at the story of the murder, that she quickly turned to society gossip and began to read, drinking coffee slowly, her eyes myopically narrowed. She would never wear glasses. "Oh, there's going to be a big party tonight at Chevy Chase . . . for . . . oh, for Heaven's sake, for Alma Edderdale I wonder what *she's* doing in Washington."

I said that I didn't know, adding, however, that whenever there was a great party Alma, Lady Edderdale—the meat king's daughter and a one-time Marchioness—was sure to be on hand. I had been to several of her parties in New York the preceding season, and very grand they were, too.

"Let's go," said Ellen suddenly.

"Go where?"

"To Chevy Chase, tonight."

"If I remember my English literature, Chevy Chase was the title of a celebrated poem by . . ."

"The Chevy Chase *Club*," said Ellen, picking up the paper again and studying the Edderdale item. "Everyone goes there . . . ah, Mrs. Goldmountain is giving the party. We must go."

"But we can't."

"And why not?" She arranged the newspaper on a silver rack to the right of her plate. "You know perfectly well why not." I was irritated, not by her lack of feeling, but by her want of good sense. "It would be a real scandal . . . murdered Senator's daughter attends party."

"Oh, I doubt that. Besides, people don't go into mourning like they used to. Anyway, *I'm* going." And that was that. I agreed finally to escort her, *if* she wore black and didn't make herself conspicuous. She promised.

90

Just as I was having my second cup of coffee, Walter Langdon appeared in the dining-room, wearing a blazer and uncreased flannels, giving one the impression that he was very gently born . . . some time during the last century. His freckled face and red hair slicked down with water, provided an American country-boy look, however.

"Hi," said the journalist of the Left Wing, taking his place beside Ellen. She smiled at him seraphically . . . how well I knew that expression: *you* are the one. Despite all the others, experienced and cynical as I am, my pilgrim soul has been touched at last . . . lover, come back to me . . . this is it. That look which had appeared over more breakfast-tables after more premières than I or any decent man could calculate. *It,* as Ellen euphemistically would say, had happened.

"Anything in the Press?" said the Left Wing, glancing shyly at his seductress.

"A wonderful party, dear . . . we're going . . . you and I and Peter. Mrs. Goldmountain is giving it for darling Alma Edderdale . . . you know the meat-packer bag who married old Edderdale."

"But. . . ." Walter Langdon, like the well-brought-up youth he was, went through the same maze of demurs as had I, with the same result. He, too, would join us at the Chevy Chase Club that night . . . and Ellen would wear black, she vowed. She surrendered the paper to Langdon, who read about the murder eagerly.

Ellen reminisced somewhat bawdily on the career of Alma Edderdale while I pretended to listen, my thoughts elsewhere, in the coffin there with Cæsar . . . and I recalled again Walter Langdon's quotation about the serpent's egg. Could Walter Langdon have killed the Senator? Unlikely, yet stranger things had happened. He was very earnest, one might even say dedicated. He had had the opportunity . . . but then everyone had had an opportunity. This was not going to be a case of *how,* but of *why,* and except for Pomeroy there weren't too many strong *whys* around. I decided that during the day I would concentrate on motives.

The Pomeroys arrived for breakfast and I avoided Mr. Pomeroy's gaze somewhat guiltily, expecting to see the cuckold's horns, like the noble antlers of some aboriginal moose, sprouting from his brow. But if he had any suspicions he did not show them, while she was a model for the adulterous wife: calm, casual, competent for any crisis . . . the four Cs. I decided that it was time someone wrote a handbook for adulterers, a nicely printed brochure containing the names of road-houses and hotels catering to illegal vice, as well as the names of those elusive figures who specialise in operations of a crucial and private nature . . . operations known as appendectomies in Hollywood and café society. I remembered the time one of the great ladies of the Silver Screen was rushed to the hospital with what an inept member of my profession, her Press agent, called a ruptured appendix, unaware that his predecessor of six months before had also announced the removal of her appendix . . . there were repercussions all the way from Chasen's to "21": and of course the lady was in even greater demand afterwards, such being the love of romance in our seedy world.

While I pondered these serious topics, there was a good deal of desultory talk at the table on sleep: who had slept how well the preceding night, and why. It seemed that Mr. Pomeroy always slept like a top, in his own words, because of a special brew of warm milk, malt and phenobarbital.

"I'm so lucky," said Camilla, "I don't need a thing to make me sleep." Nothing but a good hot . . . water-bottle, I murmured to myself, behind my coffee-cup.

Verbena Pruitt swung into the room like a sail-boat coming about in a regatta. She boomed heartily at us. "Clear morning, clear as a bell," she tolled, taking her place at the head of the table where the Senator had always sat. Cross-conversations began, and before I knew it I found myself staring into the dark dreamy eyes of Camilla Pomeroy. We talked quietly to one another, unnoticed by all the others . . . except Ellen, who noticed everything and smirked broadly at me.

"I . . . I'm so sorry," said Camilla, looking down at her plate shyly . . . as though expecting to find two-fifty there.

"Sorry?" I made a number of barking noises, very manly and gallant.

"About last night. I don't know *what* came over me." She glanced sharply across the table to see if her husband was listening; he was engrossed in an argument with Verbena Pruitt about the coming Nominating Conventions. "I've never done anything like that before," she said softly, spacing the words with care so that I would get the full impact. I thought for some reason of a marvellous army expression: it was like undressing in a warm room. I was in a ribald mood, considering the earliness of the hour.

"I guess," I whispered, "that it was just one of those things."

"You see, I'm *not* like that really."

I barked encouragingly.

"It's this *tension*," she said, and the dark eyes grew wide. "This *horrible* tension. First, Lee's death . . . then the will, that *dreadful* will." She shut her eyes a moment as though trying to forget a millions dollars . . . since this is not easily done, she opened them again. "There . . . there's nothing in the papers about it, is there?"

"Not yet. This afternoon."

"I don't know how I shall live through it. I didn't tell you last night, but the reporters have been after me . . . I don't know *how* they find out about such things, but they knew immediately. This morning one of them actually got through to me on the phone and asked for an interview, on how it felt to be . . . in a position like this." She was obviously excited by all the attention; at the same time, under the mechanical expressions of woe, I sensed a real disturbance: if ever a woman was near hysteria it was Camilla Pomeroy, but why?

I told her that the next few days would have to be lived through, the sort of reassurance which irritates me, but seems to do other people good, especially those who do not listen to what you say . . . and she never listened to anyone.

"I also wish," she said slowly, "that you would forget everything I said last night."

Before I could comment on this unusual turn of affairs, Mrs. Rhodes, a sad figure in black, entered the room and we all rose respectfully until she was seated. Conversation became general and very formal.

When breakfast was over, I went into the drawing-room to see if I had any mail. The mail was always placed on a silver tray near the fireplace . . . a good place for it: you could toss the bills directly on the fire without opening them. Needless to say, there was a pile of letters: the guests were all busy people involved in busy affairs. I glanced at all the letters, from force of habit: condolences seemed the order of the day for Mrs. Rhodes. There were no letters for Ellen, or Miss Pruitt whose office was at Party Headquarters.

There were a half-dozen letters for me, three of which went into the fireplace unopened. Of the others, one was from Miss Flynn, suggesting that my presence in New

York at my office would be advisable considering the fact that the dog I had produced for my dog-food concern had been sick on television while being interviewed and it looked as if I would lose the account. This was serious but at the moment there was nothing I could do about it.

The other letter was a chatty one from the editor at the *Globe*, commenting on the two pieces I had done for them and suggesting that I jazz my pieces up a little, that unless I produced some leads, the public would cease to read the *Globe* for news of this particular murder, in which case, I might not get the handsome sum we had decided upon earlier for my services. This was not good news at all. Somehow or other we would have to keep the case on fire, and there was no fire: a lot of smoke and a real blaze hidden somewhere, but where? Three days had passed. Pomeroy was thought to be the murderer, yet the police were unable to arrest him. There was no evidence. Despite the hints by several columnists, the public was in the dark about everything and, not wanting to risk a libel suit, I could hardly take the plunge and inform the constituents of the *Globe* that Pomeroy was the likeliest candidate for the electric chair.

Worried, exasperated, I opened the third letter.

"Boom! Rufus Hollister. Another boom? Maybe not. Maybe so. Repeat, Rufus Hollister. Paper-chase leads to him. Who's got the papers?" The note was unsigned. It was printed in red pencil on a sheet of typewriter paper. The letters slanted oddly from left to right, as though someone had deliberately tried to disguise his handwriting. I sat down by the fire, stunned.

"What's the matter, Peter?" asked Ellen, coming into view, "Camilla hurt your feelings?"

"Nothing's the matter," I said, folding the letter: I had decided, in a flash, to tell no one about it, not even Winters.

If someone wanted to give me a lead I wasn't the man to share it, 'if it be a sin to covet honour' and all that.

"Well, I'm off, with Walter. We're going to see the Senate in session . . . God knows why. We'll pick you up after dinner tonight. I've told Mother a number of white lies to explain our absence."

"What about Winters? Did you get his permission?"

"Didn't you hear? He's not going to be around at all today. Somebody called up from the police department and said he was busy. But he'll be with us again tomorrow. Walter, get my coat, will you, like a dear? It's in the hall cupboard." And talking of this and that, she left, the obedient Walter knotted loosely around her neck.

I was about to go upstairs and get my own overcoat, when Mrs. Rhodes suddenly appeared from the dining-room. It was her first visit to the drawing-room since the reading of the will; she had kept hidden, since then, except for meals. I felt very sorry for her.

"Ah, Mr. Sargeant," she smiled wanly. "Don't get up." She sat down opposite me. The fire burned merrily. The butler moved silently about the room; except for him, we were alone: our fellow suspects had all gone on about their business.

"I suspect this is more than you bargained for," she said almost apologetically. The old diamonds gleamed against her mourning.

"It's been a shock," I said . . . it was the phrase we all used to discuss what had happened.

"We must all bear it as best we can. I . . . she paused as though uncertain whether or not she could go on; she was a most reserved lady, lacking in that camaraderie so many politicians' wives assume. "I was not prepared for the will. I don't understand how Lee could . . . have made it." This was odd; she was not concerned at his having had an illegitimate child, only that he had allowed the world to know it.

"I don't suppose he expected to . . . die so soon," I said.

"Even so there was Ellen to think of, and his good name, his posterity . . . and me. Though I never expected to outlive him." She played with her rings; then she looked up at me sharply: "Will you write about the will?"

I hadn't expected a question so blunt; until now my dual rôle as suspect and journalist had not been referred to by anyone but Camilla even though all of them knew by now that I was covering the case for the *Globe*. "I suppose I'll have to," I said unhappily. I decided not to mention that I had already written about it in some detail, that my somewhat lurid version would be on the streets of New York in a few hours.

She nodded. "I realise you have a job too," she said charitably. I felt like a villain, living in her house and exposing her private life to the world, but it couldn't be helped. If I didn't do the dirty work someone else would. As a matter of fact others *were* doing it, their inaccurate reports delighting tabloid readers all over the country. She understood all this perfectly: she hadn't spent a life in the limelight for nothing.

And since you must write about these things, I think I should tell you that Camilla, though born out of wedlock, was, in a sense, legitimate. Her mother was my husband's common-law wife . . . a well-kept secret, considering the publicness of our lives. When he went into politics he married me, leaving Camilla's mother—leaving her pregnant as he learned later—only it was too late of course to do anything about that after *we* were married. Happily, the unfortunate woman, taking a sensible view of the whole business, got herself a husband as quickly as possible, an

97

undertaker named Wentworth. She died a few years later and the story, we thought, was finished."

"But didn't Camilla know who her father was?"

"Not for many years. Wentworth suspected the truth, however; he approached my husband . . . now, what I am telling you is in absolute confidence: some of it you can use. I'll tell you later what I want told to the public . . . Wentworth tried to blackmail my husband, in a cautious way. First, this favour; then, that favour. We sent his nephews to West Point. We got his brother-in-law a post office . . . the usual favours. Then his demands became unreasonable and my husband refused to fulfill them. Wentworth came to me and told me the story of Camilla which is how *I* learned the truth. He threatened to tell everyone, but by then Lee would not be budged; he was like a rock when his mind was made up. Wentworth told Camilla the truth and she left him, left his house and went to work; she supported herself until she married Roger."

"Did Wentworth spread the word after that?"

"He did, but it was useless. Those things have a habit of backfiring, you know. Most of the newspapers back home were for Lee and they wouldn't print Wentworth's rumours, and since there was no proof of any sort, it was his word against Lee's. In one of the campaigns the story of Camilla was used to smear us but the other party got nowhere with it. When one of our papers came to us and asked what they should do about these rumours, Lee said: 'Print the truth.' I think his stand won him the election." She was very proud of that frightful husband of hers. In a way, I couldn't blame her. He *had* been like a rock, very strong and proud.

"I want you," she said firmly, "to print the truth: that Camilla was his daughter by a common-law wife and that, considering the circumstances, he was in every way a good father, even to remembering her equally in his will with our daughter and with me."

"I'll do that," I said humbly, hardly able to contain my excitement at this coup. So far no journalist had bothered to check the Senator's early years.

"I will appreciate it," she said gravely.

"Tell me,' I said, suddenly brave, "who killed the Senator?"

"If only I knew." She looked bleakly into the fire. "I have no idea. I don't dare think . . . it's all so like a *paper-chase.*"

2

The idea was outageous, but who else? A paper-chase. She was trying to give me a signal of some kind, a desperate attempt at communication because. . . . because she was terrified . . . of the murderer? I wondered, though, why, if she *had* written me that note, she had not admitted it outright instead of referring so obliquely to it. A paper-chase: that was exactly it. I was suddenly very tired. If only one person would stop playing his game long enough to tell the truth, I might be able to unravel the whole business to the delight of the *Globe* and the police. That she had written to me, I was sure. But for some reason she didn't wish to be more explicit. Well, I would have to continue in the dark a while longer. In any case I was better off than I had been. I knew a good deal more about the Senator's youthful indiscretions than anyone else and I had been warned about Rufus Hollister.

After my talk with Mrs. Rhodes, I put on my overcoat and left the house. The day was bright and cold and a sharp wet wind blew down Massachusetts Avenue, making my ears ache.

99

The plain-clothes man at the door looked at me gloomily as I went out, his nose nearly as red from the cold as his ear-muffs. I saluted him airily and headed down the avenue as though I knew in which direction I was going.

Just as I was about to hail a taxi, a young man stepped from behind a tree and said, with a big smile: "I'm from the Global News-service and I wonder . . ."

"I'm from the *New York Globe,*" I said solemnly. This brought him to a full stop. He was about to walk off. Then he changed his mind.

"How come you were inside there if you're on the *Globe*? They haven't let any reporters in since the old bastard was blown up."

I explained to him.

"Oh, I know about you," he said. "You're one of the suspects. The Senator's public relations man."

I said that I had been the latter, that I doubted if I was the former.

"Well, anyway, the big arrest is going to take place soon." He sounded very confident.

"Is that so?"

"So we were tipped off . . . some time in the next twenty-four hours Winters is going to arrest the murderer. That's why I'm hanging around . . . death-watch."

"Did they tell you who he was going to arrest?" (I would rather say 'whom', but my countrymen dislike such fine points of grammar.)

"Damned if I know. Pomeroy, I suppose. Say, I wonder if you could do me a favour. You see . . ." I took care of him and his favour in a few well-chosen words. Then I caught a taxicab and rode down to the Senate Office Building.

This was my second visit to the Senator's office: it was very unlike the first. Large wooden crates filled with excelsior were placed everywhere on the floor. Two grey little women were busy packing them with the contents of the filing cabinets. I asked for Mr. Hollister and was shown into the Senator's old office. He was seated at the desk studying some documents. When I entered he looked up so suddenly that his glasses fell off.

"Ah," he sounded relieved. He retrieved his glasses and waved me to a chair beside his own. "A sad business," he said, patting the papers on the desk. "The effects," he added. There was a long pause. "You wanted to see me?" he said at last.

I nodded. I was playing the game with great care. "I thought I'd drop by and see you while I was downtown . . . to say good-bye, in a way."

"Good-bye?" The owl-eyes grew round.

"Yes, I expect I'll be going back to New York tomorrow . . . and since there'll probably be quite a bit of commotion tonight we might not have a chance to talk before then."

"I'm afraid . . ."

"They are going to make the arrest tonight." I looked at him directly. His face did not change expression but his hands suddenly stopped their patting of the papers; he made two fists; the knuckles whitened. I watched everything.

"I assume you know whom they will arrest?"

"Don't you?"

"I do not."

"Pomeroy." I wondered whether or not I had ruined the game; it was hard to tell.

He smiled suddenly, his cheeks rosy and dimpled. "Do they have all the evidence they need?"

"It would seem so."

"I hope they do because they will be terribly embarrassed

if they're not able to make it stick. I'm a lawyer, you know, and a very thorough one, if I say so myself. I would *never* go into court without ultimate proof, no sirree, I wouldn't. I hope that Lieutenant is not being rash."

"You don't think Pomeroy did it, do you?"

"I didn't say that." He spoke too quickly; then, more slowly: "I mean, it would be unfortunate if they were unprepared; the murderer might get away entirely, if that was the case."

"And you wouldn't like to see that?"

"Would you?" He was very bland. "You forget, Mr. Sargeant, that it is not pleasant for any of us to be suspected of murder. Even you are suspected, in theory at least. I am, certainly, and all the family is, too. None of us like it. We would all like to see the case done with, but if it isn't taken care of properly then we are worse off than before. Frankly, something like this can do us all great harm, Mr. Sargeant."

"I'm sure of that." I sat back in my chair and looked at the bare patch on the wall over the mantelpiece where the cartoon had been. Then I fired my last salvo: "Where are those papers you took from the study the other night? The night you shoved me downstairs?"

Hollister gasped faintly; he adjusted his glasses as though steadying them after an earthquake. "Papers?"

"Yes, the ones you were looking for. I assume you found them."

"I think your attempt at humour is not very successful, Mr. Sargeant." His composure was beginning to return and my shock-treatment had, to all intents and purposes, failed. I looked at him coolly, however, and waited. "I did *not* take the papers," he said, smiling. "I admit that I should have liked to, but someone else got them."

"You are sure of that?"

Hollister chuckled but his eyes were round and hard

despite his smiling mouth. "Perfectly sure." At that moment the telephone rang; he picked it up and talked to some newspaper-man, very sharply, I thought, for someone in public life; but then his public life was over, at least as far as the Senate was concerned. "Wolves!" he groaned, hanging up.

"Closing in for the kill."

"Closing in for what?"

"The arrest . . . tonight, I am told."

Hollister shook his head gloomily. "Poor man. I can't think why he did it; but then he has a most vindictive nature, and a terrible temper. He depended a great deal on the Senator's backing in Washington. It was probably too much for him to bear, being turned down like that."

"I have a hunch that there will be a good deal of singing, though, as the gangsters say." I was beginning to talk out of the side of my mouth, the way private eyes are meant to talk. I caught myself in time: this was, as far as I could recall, the first time in my life I had used the word 'singing' in its underworld sense.

Mr. Hollister looked properly bewildered. "I mean," I said, "that in the course of the trial a lot of very dirty linen is going to be displayed. I mean, Mr. Hollister, that all your political dealings with the Senator will become known." This was wild; I forged ahead in the dark. "The papers you wanted and which you say someone else got will be very embarrassing for all concerned." I was proud of my emphatic vagueness; also of the effect I was making.

"What are you trying to tell me, Sargeant?" The soft-soap political manner was succeeded by an unsuspected brusqueness. He was near the end of the line.

"That Pomeroy is going to tear you to pieces."

Hollister half rose in his chair; before he could speak, the telephone rang again. He picked it up impatiently; then his manner changed. He was suddenly mild. "Yes, yes. I certainly will. Anything you say. Yes. Midnight? Fine. Yes. . . ." His voice trailed off into a series of "yeses" accompanied by little smiles, lost on his caller. When he hung up, he changed moods again. "I'm sorry, Mr. Sargeant, but I have a great deal of work to do, packing up the Senator's papers and all. I don't know if you've heard the news but Governor Ledbetter has just appointed himself to succeed to the Senator's unfilled term and we're expecting him tomorrow. Good afternoon."

3

The Chevy Chase Club is a large old-fashioned building outside Washington, in Maryland. There is a swimming-pool, a fine golf-course, lawns, big trees, a lovely vista complete with fireflies in the early evening, in season; but we were not in season and my information as to the fireflies and so on was provided by Ellen as we taxied from Washington to the Club. She waxed nostalgic, relating episodes from her youth: in the pool, on the courts, on the course, even on the grass among the trees, though the presence of the innocent Langdon spared us a number of unsavoury details.

We had had no trouble getting away that evening, to my surprise. Mrs. Rhodes was properly hoodwinked and the Lieutenant, when we called him to ask permission to go off for the evening, gave it easily. The arrest was going to be made after all, I decided. I wondered if I should leave the dance early so that I could be on hand for the big event. Langdon and Ellen would doubtless be so absorbed in one another that my early departure would not be noticed.

Ellen looked almost regal in her black evening-gown. I

had never seen her in a black evening-dress before, and she was a most striking figure. Her tawny hair pulled straight back from her face like a Roman matron's and her pale shoulders bare beneath a sable stole. Langdon wore a blue suit and I wore a tuxedo; I had arrived in Washington all prepared for a real social whirl.

The Club was a handsome building with high ceilings and great expanses of polished floor. It had a summery atmosphere even though snow was on the ground outside and the night was bitter cold.

The gathering looked very distinguished . . . half a thousand guests at least, in full evening-dress. Poor Langdon blushed and mumbled about his blue serge suit but Ellen swept us into the heart of the party without a moment's hesitation.

Mrs Goldmountain was a small woman of automatic vivacity, very dark, ageless, with exquisite skin carefully painted and preserved. I recognised her from afar: her picture was always in the magazines smiling up into the President's face or the Vice-President's face or into her dog's face, a celebrated white poodle which was served its meals at its own table beside hers on all state occasions: "Because Hermione loves interesting people," so the newspapers had quoted her as saying. Whether Hermione Poodle liked famous people or not, we shall never know; that Mrs. Goldmountain did, however, is one of the essential facts about Washington, and famous people certainly liked *her* because she made a fuss over them, gave rich parties where they met other celebrities. One of the laws of nature is that celebrities adore one another . . . are, in fact, more impressed by the idea of celebrity than the average indifferent citizen who never see a movie star and seldom bothers to see his Congressman, presuming he knows what a Congressman is. I looked about me for the

poodle but she was nowhere in sight: the dream no doubt
of a press agent. Mrs. Goldmountain retained several.

"Ellen Rhodes! Ah, poor darling!" Mrs. Goldmountain
embraced her greedily, her little black eyes glistening with
interest: this was a coup for her. We were presented and
each received a blinding smile, the dentures nearly as bright
as the famous Goldmountain emeralds which gleamed at
her throat like a chain of 'Go' lights. Mr. Goldmountain
had been very rich; he had, also, been gathered up some
years ago . . . or ridden on ahead, as my Miss Flynn would
also say . . . leaving his fortune to his bride.

"I am so touched, poor angel," said Mrs. G., holding both
of Ellen's hands tight in hers and looking intently into her
face. "I know how much you cared for your poor father."

"I wanted to see you," said Ellen simply, the lie springing
naturally to her coral lips.

"Your mother? Shattered?"

"Utterly . . . we all are."

"Oh, it's too horrible."

"Too."

"And the Chief Justice told me only yesterday that he
might well have got the nomination."

"Ah!"

"What a President he would have been. . . . How we
shall miss him! all of us. I wanted terribly to get to the
funeral, but the Marchioness of Edderdale and the Elector
of Saxe-Weimar were both visiting me and we could hardly
get away. I sent flowers."

"Mother was so grateful."

"Darling, I couldn't be more upset and you *are* an angel
to come. . . ." Then she began to speak very rapidly, looking over our shoulders at an Ambassador who was arriving
with his retinue, their ribbons and orders gleaming
discreetly. Before we knew it we were cut adrift as the

high enthusiastic voice of our hostess fired a volley of compliments and greetings at the Ambassador and his outriders.

"*That* is over," said Ellen, in a cool competent voice and she led us to the bar; the guests parted before our determined way. Those who recognised her looked surprised and murmured condolences and greetings; then mild complaints at her lack of rectitude when we had passed on. I caught only a few words here and there: mostly disparaging.

The bar was a panelled room, a little less crowded than the main hall. From the ballroom could be heard the sound of a very smooth orchestra playing something with a lot of strings.

"Now isn't this better than being cooped up in that awful house?" said Ellen blithely, clutching a Scotch in her strong predatory fingers.

"Of course it is," I said. But . . ." And mechanically I reminded her that she was making an unfavourable impression.

"Who cares? Besides, I always do and everyone adores it: gives them something to talk about." She smoothed her hair back, though not a strand was out of place. She was easily the best-looking woman in the room and there were, for some reason, more women in the bar than men, Washington women being, perhaps, a trifle more addicted to the grape than their menfolk: the result of the tedium of their lives, no doubt, the dreary round of protocol-ridden days.

Walter Langdon then wanted to know who was who and while Ellen explained to him, I wandered off to the ballroom.

Beneath tall paintings of old gentlemen in hunting costume, the politicos danced. I recognised the Marchioness of Edderdale, a Chicago meat-man's girl who had bought a number of husbands, one of whom was the ill-starred Marquis of Edderdale who had got caught in the rigging of his schooner during a regatta some years ago and was hanged, in the presence of royalty, too. The Marchioness whose present name no one bothered with, the title being so much more interesting, stood vaguely smiling at the guests who were presented to her and to the Vice-President of the United States who was drinking champagne beside her and telling, no doubt, one of his celebrated stories. I made my way over to her and presented my compliments.

"Ah, Mr. . . ." She gestured handsomely.

"Sargeant," I said and quickly reminded her of my last visit to her house. She recalled it, too.

"I hope you will come see me soon,' she said. "Mr. Sargeant, this is . . ." And she paused; she had forgotten the Vice-President's name. I quickly shook his hand murmuring how honoured I was, saving the dignity of the the nation. It occurred to me that she might not have known who he was either: her world after all was New York and the south of France, Capri, and London in the month of June, not Washington and the unimportant world of politics.

The Vice-President began a story and, by the time he had got to the end of it, a large group of politicans and climbers had surrounded us and I was able to creep away, my brush with history ended. Just as I reached the outskirts of the party, a familiar figure crossed my line of vision, heading towards the great man. The familiar figure stopped when he saw me and a wide smile broke his florid hearty face. It was Elmer Bush, renowned commentator and columnist ("This is Elmer Bush, bringing you news while it's news."). We had been on the *Globe* together; or at least he had been a star columnist when I was the assistant drama critic. In the ballet murder case I had managed completely to undo his foul machinations. He had been of the opinion that my young woman of the time, a dancer, was the killer and he had presented her to the public as such. I scooped him, in every sense, and as a result we had not seen each other, by design, since.

Bygones were now allowed to be bygones, however.

"Peter Sargeant, well, isn't this a surprise?" My hand was gripped firmly, the sun-lamp-tanned face broke into a number of genial triangles; the bloodshot blue eyes gleamed with whisky and insincere good-fellowship. I loathe Elmer Bush.

"How are you, Elmer," I said quietly, undoing my hand from his.

"Top of the world. Looks like us country boys are travelling in real society, doesn't it?" Which meant of course: what the hell are you doing here, you little squirt?

"Always go first-class," I mumbled, wondering what he had in mind, why he was in Washington.

"You talking to the Vice-President?"

I nodded casually. "He was telling a story. It seems there was a farmer who . . ."

Elmer laughed loudly. "Know it well," he said, before I could get started. I had intended to bore the life out of him with it. "Marvellous old devil, marvellous. Say, I saw your by-line the other day."

I nodded gravely.

"Didn't know you were still in the game. Thought you were mostly involved in publicity."

"I am," I said. "This was just one of those things."

"Rhodes hired you, didn't he?"

"Couple days before he died."

"I may drop by and see you . . . living in the house, aren't you?" I nodded. "Terrible tragedy," he said thoughtfully, the Vice-President still in focus in the background, me slightly out of focus in the foreground since the eyes can't look two places at once. "I thought I might do a programme about the case. You might like to be on it. I'm on television now, coast to coast."

I said that I knew all about this, that I probably wouldn't be able to go on television and that he probably would not be allowed to visit the house since all newspaper people were rigidly excluded. I was on to him: he was ready to move in, positive that for a half-hour's display of my pretty face to the television audience of America, I would give him the beat on the murder. Not a chance in the world, Brother Bush, I vowed.

"Mrs. Rhodes is an old friend of mine," said Elmer, with a hurt expression. "The Senator and I were very close, very. Well, I suspect young Winters will be able to fix it for me, unless he's too busy with the arrest."

This was unexpected, but then Elmer Bush was no fool; he was still a first-rate newspaper-man, despite his sickening hopespun television manner. He had already closed in on Winters, who was doubtless giving him all the information he needed. All he needed me for was to get to know the family, and to get me side-tracked along the way.

"Arrest?" I looked surprised.

"Pomeroy . . . tonight . . . that's the word. Matter of fact, I plan to get down to the police station about one o'clock to see him booked." Then Elmer was gone to join the group around the Vice-President.

This gave me pause. Thoughtfully I made my way to the men's room, a large locker-room, as it turned out. I was meditating on what to do next when I noticed that Walter Langdon was standing beside me.

"Nice party?" I asked.

He beamed foolishly. "Just fine," he said. He sounded a little drunk.

"Ellen having a good time?"

"Doesn't she always? She's dancing with some Ambassador or other now."

"Jilted you already?"

"Oh no." He missed the humour of my remark. "She's just having a good time."

"I suppose you'll be publishing the banns soon."

"How did you know?" He turned very red and I felt like kicking him for being such a baby. Instead I arranged my garments and departed, leaving him to his dreams among the tile and enamel.

I glanced at my watch. It was eleven-forty. At twelve I would go back to the house, alone. Langdon could manage Ellen by himself; if he couldn't, well, it was his business now.

I danced a few times with various ladies, all belonging to the embassies of South American Powers, dark vital girls devoted to dancing.

I saw Ellen only once, whirling by in the arms of a sturdy Marine officer. She gave me her devil-leer, over his bulging arm. That might very well be the end of little Walter, I thought, extricating myself from the last Latin girl under pretext of having to join my wife.

Shortly before midnight, Hermione, a large precious-looking white poodle, made her appearance. After being introduced to the more interesting people, she sang, rather badly, while the orchestra played what accompaniment it could. There was a great deal of applause when she finished and Hermione was given a sherry flip. Thinking of the decline of Rome, I left the club, bowing first to Mrs. Goldmountain, who, under the impression that I was a new Congressman, said she would see me at the House Office one day soon when she paid the Speaker a call.

Since neither Ellen nor Langdon was in sight, I left without telling them of my plans. Actually, I preferred to be alone at this stage of the game. We were approaching a climacteric, as Mr. Churchill would say, and I was becoming tense. I took one of the fleet of taxis in front of the club, and set out for Washington.

For some reason I expected to find the house blazing with light and crowded with television cameras while Pomeroy, shrieking vengeance, handcuffed to Lieutenant Winters, awaited the Black Maria.

Instead everything was as usual. The plain-clothes man still stood guard and no more lights were on than usual.

In the drawing-room, I found Mrs. Rhodes and Verbena Pruitt. Both looked quite shaken.

"Has it happened?"

Miss Pruitt nodded, her chin vanishing into its larger fellows. "They took Roger away half an hour ago."

I sat down heavily opposite them. "Roger!" said Mrs. Rhodes, but I could not tell whether or not she spoke with sorrow or anger or fright. I fixed myself a drink.

"Where is Mrs. Pomeroy?" I asked.

"She's gone to the police station with him. Brave girl. But then it's a woman's place to be beside her mate when dark days come," announced Miss Pruitt in a voice not unlike her usual political manner. She talked for several minutes about the ideal relationship between man and wife, not in the least embarrassed by her own maidenhood.

"Then it's all over?" I asked.

Mrs. Rhodes closed her eyes. "I hope so," she murmured.

Miss Pruitt shook her head vigorously; hairpins flew dangerously across the room. "They have to *prove* it," she said. "Until then we *all* have to be on hand. God knows how long it will take."

"We won't have to stay here during the trial?" I was becoming alarmed.

"No, just the preliminaries . . . Grand Jury . . . indictment. Then we can go. Even so, it means the rest of the week is shot."

"I always liked Roger," said Mrs. Rhodes thoughtfully, looking into the fire.

"The whole thing is a bad dream," said Miss Pruitt, with finality.

"I'm sure he would never have done such a thing."

"Then who *would've* done it? Not I, nor you, nor this boy, nor Ellen . . . and I doubt if that newspaper-boy or Rufus or Camilla would have done it. Of course I will admit that *I* suspect the servants, especially that butler. Oh, I know how fond you are of him and how devoted he is *supposed* to be to you, but let me tell you that on more than one occasion domestics of unimpeachable character have been found to be murderers, and why? because of this habit of leaving them money. Think how many old ladies are undoubtedly murdered by their beloved companions for money, for a small inheritance. An everyday occurrence, believe you me." Verbena Pruitt rattled on; Mrs. Rhodes stared at the fire. Neither asked me what I was doing in evening clothes. Ellen had not been missed either, or if she had neither mentioned it.

Soon they left the drawing-room and went to bed. The moment I was alone, I telephoned Winters. To my surprise I was put through to him. He sounded very lively.

"I suppose it's all over?" For some reason my voice had a most lugubrious ring.

"That's right. We've arrested Pomeroy."

"Has he confessed?"

"No, and doesn't seem to have any intention of confessing. Won't make any difference, though."

"Then I can say that Lieutenant Winters has sufficient

evidence on hand to justify his dramatic arrest of the chief suspect?"

"That's right." Winters sounded very happy about the whole thing. I contributed to his happiness by indicating that as a reward for giving me the news first, I would see that he was liberally rewarded with space and applause in the *Globe*. He assured me that no other journalist had been informed as yet: a number of newspaper people had collected at the police station, but so far he had made no statement; I was getting the news first, for which I thanked him, although the *Globe* is an afternoon paper and would, if the morning papers were sufficiently alert, be scooped. Still, I had the whole story.

"By the way, what are you building your case on?" This seemed like a fair question; one which would doubtless be evaded.

It was. "I can't say yet. There's enough circumstantial evidence, though, to make the story. Just say the police have the affair in hand."

"Is Mrs. Pomeroy at the station?"

"Yes. She's talking to her husband; they're waiting for their lawyer to arrive."

"Is she pale but dry-eyed?"

"I haven't looked."

"Who, by the way, is the lawyer?"

"The new Senator . . . the Governor. He just got in from Talisman City."

"Is *he* going to handle the case?" I was surprised. Senator did not, as far as I knew, handle criminal cases.

"No, he's going to direct the legal operations, though. We're not worried." And on a note of confidence, our interveiw closed.

Now all that was left was to write the story. I picked up a pad of paper with the legend "U.S. Senate" across the top and then, with a pencil, I began to sketch out my story for the *Globe*. I had lot to record. The story Mrs. Rhodes had told me about the childhood of Camilla Pomeroy; a description of the relations between the Senator and the accused; a perfervid account of the arrest and Pomeroy, pale but dry-eyed, being led away by the police, protesting his innocence.

As I took notes, however, I was aware that the case was not solved. I am not sure now, when I look back on these events, *wh*y I should have doubted that the most likely man to do the murder had done the murder. I am not one of those devious-minded souls who feel that the most obvious culprit is never the one who did the dirty work. My respect for human ingenuity is not that great. In most cases involving violence, the guilty party is also the most obvious one . . . the professional writers of mystery novels to the contrary. But Pomeroy just did not strike me as the murdering type.

Half-way through my note-taking, I stopped and looked about the room, brilliantly lit and empty. The fire burned cosily; from far away I could hear the wind. The phrase "a paper-chase" kept going through my head. Someone in the house knew who the murderer was, or suspected. Some-one had tried to give me a lead about some papers, about Rufus Hollister. The someone, I was fairly certain, was Mrs. Rhodes, a woman far less simple and direct than she appeared to be . . . a frightened woman, too. Yet the note didn't imply that Rufus was the murderer, only that he held the key to the murder, perhaps without knowing it. Papers. I frowned, but even this solemn expression did not help me much. Every time I tried to unravel the puzzle, my mind would become completely unfocused and frivolous, all sorts of irrelevancies floating about in it. There was really nothing to go on, no real facts, no clues other than the letter, only my intuition, which is, according to friends, somewhat below average and my knowledge of the characters involved which was slight, to say the least.

Yet Rufus had been up to some skulduggery with the Senator. He had, I was almost certain, made a raid on the study in the hopes of finding papers there, documents so hidden that not even the police would have been able to find them. Since it was generally known that Winters had removed all the files from the study, only someone intimately connected with the Senator's affairs would have known where to find papers hidden so well the police had not seen them. Who knew his affairs the best? Hollister and Mrs. Rhodes and, of the suspect at least, that was all. Hollister wanted something; Hollister knew where to find it; Hollister had taken a big chance and probably, got what he wanted and cleared himself.

Cleared himself of what?

I decided to embark upon the chase. I stuffed my notes into my pocket. I wouldn't have to telephone my story in to the *Globe* until dawn. By which time I might have some real news.

I went upstairs to Rufus Hollister's room. The blanket still hung at the end of the corridor, although the door behind it had been repaired and bolted shut, no longer requiring the presence of a plain-clothes man.

I knocked on Hollister's door, very softly. There was no answer. Not wanting to disturb the other sleepers, I turned the knob and pushed the door open.

Hollister was seated at his desk, apparently hard at work.

I shut the door softly behind me; then, since he had made no move, I walked over to his desk and said: "I wonder if . . ." But the sight of blood stopped me.

Great quantities of blood covered his face, his shirt, the

desk in front of him; only the typewriter was relatively clear of it.

He was dead, of course, shot through the right temple. The gun, a tiny pearl-handled affair, lay on the floor beside his right hand; it gleamed dully in the lamplight.

My first impulse was to run as far as I could from this room. My second impulse was to shout for the plainclothes man out front. My third impulse, and the one which I followed, was to make a search of the room.

I was surprised at my own calm as I touched his hand to see if *rigor mortis* had set in: it had not. He was only recently dead. I looked at my watch to check on the time: one-nineteen. I looked at *his* watch, recalling how watches were supposed to stop magically when the wearer died . . . this watch was ticking merrily: about five minutes fast, too.

I don't know why it took me so long to notice the confession which was still in the typewriter.

"I killed Senator Rhodes on Wednesday, the 13th, by placing a package of explosive in his fireplace shortly after we returned from the Senate Office Building Tuesday afternoon. Rather than see an innocent man be condemned for my crime I herewith make this confession. As to my reason for killing the Senator, I prefer not to say, since a complete confession would implicate others. I will say, though, that we were involved in an illegal business operation which failed. Because of the coming election, the Senator saw fit to make me the victim of that failure . . . which would have involved a jail sentence for me and the ruin of my reputation. Rather than suffer this, I took the occasion of Pomeroy's visit to Washington to kill the Senator, throwing guilt on Pomeroy. Unfortunately I was not able to discover the documents pertaining to our business venture. They are either in the hands of the police or shortly will be. I have no choice but to take this way out, since I prefer dying to a jail sentence and the ruin of my career. I feel no remorse, however. I killed in self-defence. Rufus Hollister." The name was typewritten but not signed; as though immediately after typing this confession he had shot himself, without even pulling the paper out of the typewriter.

Well, this was more than I had bargained for. The paper-chase had led me to a corpse, and to the answer.

Methodically, I searched the room. As far as I could tell, there was nothing else to add or subtract from what had happened. The case, it would seem, was closed. With a handkerchief I carefully wiped any prints I might have made on the watch and wrist of the corpse (I had touched nothing else); then I went downstairs and telephoned Lieutenant Winters. It was now one-thirty-six, the anniversary of the Senator's death.

FIVE

I

IT was another all-night session.

Winters nearly had a nervous breakdown that night and the rest of us were far from being serene. We were interviewed one after the other in the dining-room, just like the first night, but under more distracting circumstances, for police photographers and investigators were all over the place, and there was talk that Winters would soon be succeeded by another, presumably more canny, official. The Pomeroys returned, looking no worse than the rest of us that grizzly dawn. The newspaper people were at every window until they were finally given a somewhat muffled and confused statement by Winters. He made no mention of the arrest of Pomeroy, an arrest which had not been legally completed, I gathered, since Mr. Pomeroy was now among us.

I sat beside Ellen in the drawing-room. The others, the ones who were not being interviewed, talked quietly to one another or else dozed, like Verbena Pruitt, in her chair, her mouth open and snoring softly, her hair in curlers and her majestic *corse damascened* in an intimate garment of the night.

Ellen for once looked tired. Langdon sat some distance away, staring at the coals in the fireplace, wondering no doubt how on earth he was to get a story for *Advance-guard* out of all this confusion.

"Why," said Ellen irritably, "do they keep us up like this

if Rufus did the murder? Why all this damned questioning? Why don't they go home?"

"They have to find out where we all were," I said reasonably . . . but I wondered too why the confusion since the police had not only a confession, but the confessor's corpse, the ideal combination from the official point of view: no expensive investigation, no long-drawn-out trial, no angry Press demanding a solution and a conviction.

Through the crack between the curtains, I saw the grey dawn and heard the noise of morning traffic in the streets. My eyes twitched with fatigue.

Ellen yawned. "In a few minutes I'm going to go to bed, whether they like it or not."

"Why don't you? They've already got your testimony." There was a commotion in the hall. We both looked and saw Rufus Hollister departing by stretcher, a sheet of canvas over him. As the front door opened, there was a roar of triumph from the waiting photographers; flash-bulbs went off. The door was slammed loudly and Rufus Hollister's earthly remains were gone to their reward: the morgue, and, finally, the tomb.

"Disgusting!" said Ellen, using for the first time in my experience that censorious word. Then, without permission, she went to bed.

After the body was gone, a strange peace fell over the house. The policemen and photographers and investigators all stole quietly away, leaving the witnesses alone in the house with Winters and a guard.

At five o'clock I was admitted to the dining-room.

Winters sat with bloodshot eyes and tousled hair looking at a vast pile of testimony, all in shorthand, the work of his secretary, who sat a few feet down the table with a pad and pencil.

He grunted when I said hello; I sat down.

He asked me at what time I had found the body. I told him.

"Did you touch anything in the room?"

"Only the corpse's hand, his wrist, to see how long he was dead, or *if* he was dead."

"Was the body in the same position when we arrived that it was in when you found it?"

"Yes."

"What were you doing in Hollister's room at that time of night?" The voice, though tired, was sharp and impersonal.

"I wanted to ask him something."

"What did you want to ask him?"

"About a note I received this morning."

Winters looked at me, surprised. "A note? What note?"

I handed it to him. He read it quickly. "When did this arrive?" His voice was cold.

"This morning at breakfast . . . or rather yesterday morning."

"Why didn't you tell me about it?"

"Because I thought it was a hoax. I figured there was plenty of time to give it to you. I had no idea you were planning to arrest Pomeroy so quickly." This was a well-directed jab at the groin. Winters scowled.

"You realise that there is a penalty for withholding vital evidence?"

"I didn't withhold it. I just gave it to you."

A four-letter word of exasperation and anger burst from his classic mouth. We were both silent for a moment. He studied the letter. "What," he said in a less official voice, "do you think it means?"

"I thought it meant that Hollister was the one who broke into the library that night and got some incriminating documents, or tried to find some."

"Obviously he didn't find them."

"Did *you* find them?"

The law shook its head. "If we did we weren't aware of their significance," he said candidly. "We've checked and double-checked all the secret files and, as far as I can tell, there isn't anything in any of them which would send Hollister to jail, or even the Senator . . . a lot of fast political deals, but nothing illegal."

"Do you think the Senator might have kept his business transactions somewhere else?" I recalled those mysterious safety deposit-boxes belonging to pillars of the Congress which revealed, when opened posthumously, mysterious quantities of currency, received for services rendered.

"I think we'd have found it by now."

"Maybe the Governor might be able to tell you. He was the Senator's lawyer."

Winters sighed and looked discouraged. "I can't get a word out of him. All he does is harangue me about our heritage of civil liberty."

"Maybe you can track down who wrote that note and ask them."

Winters looked at me vindictively. "You picked a fine time to let me know, right after I almost made a false arrest. What was the big idea?"

"Remember that I didn't see you all day. I got the note in the morning. I went to see Hollister to question him . . ."

"Then you *did* talk to him about the papers?"

"I certainly did."

Winters was interested. "What did you get out of him? How did he seem?"

"I got nothing out of him, and, for a man who planned to commit suicide in the next few hours, he was remarkably calm."

"No hint at all? What exactly happened? Word for word."

I tried to recall as exactly as possible my conversation, making my bluffs sound, in the telling, more insidiously clever than they were. My testimony was recorded by the silent clerk.

When I finished the Lieutenant was no wiser. "Was anyone else there? Did he mention anyone else's name?"

"Not that I remember. We were alone. Some newspaper people tried to get him on the phone, and . . ." A light was turned on in my head, without warning. "What time did Hollister die?"

"What time . . ." Winters was too weary to react quickly.

"The coroner, what time did he fix his death?"

"Oh, about twelve. They'll know exactly when the autopsy is made."

"Hollister was murdered," I said, with a studious avoidance of melodrama, so studiously did I avoid the dramatic that Winters did not understand me. I was forced to repeat myself, my announcement losing much of its inherent grandeur with repetition.

"No," said Lieutenant Winters, beginning to weave in his chair, "he was the murderer. We have his confession."

"Which was typed by the murderer after he was shot."

"Go to bed."

"I plan to, in a few minutes. Before I go I want to make sure that you plan to keep a heavy guard in this house. I have no intention of being the next ox slaughtered."

"Why," said Winters, with a mock show of patience, "do you think Hollister was murdered?"

"Because when I was in his office yesterday morning he got a telephone-call from an unknown party who made a date to see him last night at midnight, at twelve o'clock, at the hour of his death. From what he said over the phone, I could tell it was someone he was very anxious to please . . . somone he had every intention of meeting."

"Perhaps he saw them and then killed himself."

"Not likely. Not in the house. He was home all evening, I gather. He had made no plan to go out. Therefore his guest was coming to see him here. But no one entered or left the house, as far as we know . . . no *stranger,* that is. Whoever he was supposed to meet was already in the house, one of the suspects . . . the murderer, in fact."

While I had been talking Winters sat straighter and straighter in his chair. When I paused for breath, he said: "I don't want you to say anything about this to anyone. Understand?"

"I do."

"Not only because you may be right and the murderer would be warned, but because if you are right and the murderer does think you're on his trail, we will have a third victim."

I said that I had no desire to make the front pages as a corpse.

"There's a chance you're right," he said thoughtfully. "I wish to hell you'd used your head and got that anonymous letter to me earlier. We could have tested it for prints, checked the handwriting and the paper . . . now it'll take us several days to get a report on it. In the meantime, keep your mouth shut. Pretend the case is finished, which is what we're going to do. We'll keep the house party together for a few days longer, as long as we can. We'll have to act quickly."

"I know," I said, feeling a little chilly and strange. "By the way, whose pistol was it that did the murder?"

"Mrs. Rhodes's."

I was most reluctant to meet the light the next morning, as the Roman poets would say, or rather the afternoon of the same day. I probably would have slept until evening if the telephone beside my bed hadn't rung. I picked up the receiver, eyes still closed, positive that I could continue sleeping while conducting a lively conversation on the phone.

For several moments I mumbled confidently into the receiver, aware of a far-away buzz. Then I opened one eye and saw that I was talking into the wrong end. Correcting this, completely awake, I listened to Miss Flynn's gentle reproaches.

"A Number of things have Come up," she said, "Which require your *personal* Supervision."

I explained to her that a Number of things had come up here, too, that I couldn't get away for several days.

"We were of the opinion that the case had been concluded in Washington and that the recent Suicidalist was, *ipso facto,* the Murderer of the Statesman."

"Are the papers out?" I had not realised it was so late, that the afternoon papers were already on the street.

"Indeed they are. With a Prominent Display in the *Globe* bearing your Signature."

I had pulled out all the stops in that article, just before going to bed. I had used more colours than the rainbow contains in my description of finding the body, of the case's conclusion, for that was how Winters and I wanted it to sound. The editor had been most pleased and it took considerable strength on my part not to tell him there would be yet another story.

I stalled Miss Flynn as, unhappily, she outlined the various troubles which had befallen my clients. Most of the complications were easily handled over the phone. The dog food concern offered a serious crisis, however; fortunately, I was visited with one of my early morning revelations. I told Miss Flynn to tell those shyster purveyors of horse-meat that in twenty-four hours I would have a remarkable scheme for them. She was not enthusiastic, but then enthusiasm would ill become her natural pomp.

After our conversation, I telephoned Mrs. Goldmountain and, rather to my surprise, got her. We made an appointment to meet later that afternoon.

Then I bathed, dressed, and, prepared for almost anything, went downstairs. I was a little surprised to find life proceeding so calmly. Lunch was just over and the guests were sitting about in the drawing-room. The law was nowhere in sight.

If anyone had noticed my absence during the day, it was not mentioned when I joined them.

I told the butler I wanted only coffee, which I would have in the drawing-room. Then I joined Ellen and Langdon by the window. The blinds were drawn, indicating either a bad day or the presence of police and newspaper people outside.

"Ah!" said Ellen, at my approach. She looked, of them all, the freshest. Langdon was rather grey and puffy.

"Ah, yourself." I sat down across from them. Coffee was brought me. I took a long swallow and the world at last fell into a proper perspective.

"The case," I said in Holmesian accents, "is closed."

"Not quite," said Ellen, looking at me with eyes as clear as quartz, despite the debauchery and tension of the night before. "It seems there is another day or two of questioning ahead of us, lucky creatures that we are. I've done everything except offer Winters my person to be allowed to go back to New York."

I didn't say the obvious; instead I asked her why she wanted to go back. "Tonight is Bess Pringle's party, that's why. It's going to be *the* party of the season, and I want to go."

"Why does he want us to stay here?" I pretended innocence.

"God only knows. Red tape of some kind."

"I've thought of one approach to the murder," said Langdon suddenly, emerging from a grey study.

"And that?" I tried to look interested.

"The red tape aspects. You know, the complications which a murder sets in motion, all the automatic and pointless things which must be done, the . . ." His voice began to trail off as our lack of interest became apparent. I did see how the *Advanceguard* was able to keep its circulation down to the distinguished and essential few.

Before Ellen could begin her laments about Bess Pringle or Langdon could discuss the case with me, I asked about the party, explaining my early return to the house with some ready lie.

"We didn't get back until two," said Langdon gloomily.

"And I wouldn't have come back at all if I had known what had happened," said Ellen sharply.

"Did I miss anything?"

"A member of the Cabinet played a harmonica," said Langdon coldly.

"He played a medley from Stephen Foster," said Ellen.

"I thought you were with that Marine when the concert was given," Langdon was catching on to our Ellen with considerable speed, considering his youth and idealism.

"Ah," said Ellen, and closed her eyes.

I left them and went over to the table by the fireplace where the mail was kept. There was only one letter for me, a thick one addressed in red pencil, the handwriting slanting backwards. My hands shook as I opened it.

Out fell a sheaf of legal documents. I looked through them rapidly, trying to find some explanation; there was none, no covering letter: nothing but a pile of legal documents which, without examining them, I knew concerned the business affairs of Hollister and the Senator, the papers for want of which he had apparently killed himself.

Before I could examine them further, Camilla Pomeroy came over to me, smiling gently. "How wonderful to be out of all this!" she exclaimed, looking deep into my eyes.

"You'll be going back to Talisman City soon, won't you?"

"As soon as possible," she said.

"You must be relieved," I said, trying to tell from her expression what she was actually thinking; but I could not: her face was as controlled as a bad actress'.

"Oh, terribly. Roger is like a new man."

"He was in a tough spot."

"Very!" She was not at all like the woman who had come to my room the other night with every intention not only of forbidden pleasure, but of incriminating her husband. She was again the loyal wife, incapable of treachery. What was she all about?"

"I . . . I want you to know that I wasn't myself the night we had our *talk*. I was close to a breakdown, and I'm afraid I didn't know what I was doing, or saying. You *will* forgive me, won't you?"

"There's nothing to forgive," I said gallantly, knowing perfectly well she was afraid I might let her husband know in some fashion about her betrayal, her double treachery.

"I hope you really feel that," she said softly. Then, since there was nothing else to say, I excused myself; I asked the guard at the door where Winters might be found. He gave me the address of the police headquarters, and so, without further ado, I took a taxi down-town.

I was escorted to Winters's office, an old-fashioned affair with one tall window full of dirty glass. He sat at a functional desk surrounded by filing cabinets. He was studying some papers when I entered.

"What news?" I asked.

He waved me to a chair. "No news," he said, tossing the papers aside. "A report on your note from Mr. Anonymous. The handwriting isn't identifiable, even though we have compared it to everyone's in the house . . . the paper is perfectly ordinary and like none in the house, a popular bond sold everywhere, the red pencil is an ordinary red pencil like perhaps a dozen found scattered around the house, the finger-prints on the letter are all yours. . . ."

"I didn't rub off someone else's, did I?"

"There were none to rub off. I think sometimes that it should be made illegal for movies and television to discuss finger-printing . . . since finger-printing came into fashion, practically every criminal now wears gloves, and all because they go to movies." He swore sadly to himself.

"Well, you got a good press," I said cheerfully.

"It won't be so good when it develops that someone murdered Hollister, *if* someone did."

'You don't have any doubts, do you?"

"When it comes to this case, my mind is filled with doubts about everything."

"Well, here's a bit of news." I handed him the documents.

We spent an hour going over them; neither of us was much good at reading corporation papers, but we got the general drift: a company had been formed to exploit certain oil-lands in the Senator's state. Stock had been floated; the company had been dissolved at considerable profit to the original investors; it had been reformed under another name but with the same directors; more stock had been issued; it had been merged with a dummy company belonging to the Governor of the state. The investors took a beating and only Rufus Hollister, the Governor and the late Senator profited by these elaborate goings-on. Needless to say, the whole subject was infinitely more complicated and the *New York Times'* subsequent account of the deals gives far more coherent account than I can. It was also clear that the Senator had fixed it so that he was in the clear should all this come to light and that Rufus Hollister was responsible, on paper at least, for everything; the Governor seemed in the clear, too.

Winters called in his finger-print people, also a lawyer; the papers were handed over to them for joint investigation.

"It waxes strange," I said.

"Why," said Winters, "would Mr. X want to send you these papers? And the earlier lead, if it was the same person who sent you both?"

"I suppose because he thinks I will use them properly."

"Then why not send them to the police?"

"Maybe he doesn't like policemen."

"Yet why, of all the people in the house, send it to you?" He looked at me suspiciously.

"The only person I can think of, outside of my enormous charm and intelligence, is that I am writing all this up for the *Gobe* . . . maybe the murderer is interested in a good Press. I think maybe that's the reason; then, perhaps, it doesn't make too much difference to him who gets the information since he knows it will come to the police in the end, anyway . . . it might have been just a whim . . . you have to admit the style of the first note was pretty damned whimsical."

Winters grunted and looked at the ceiling.

"A number of people have seen fit to confide in me because of my position with the Fourth Estate. I may as well tell you that Camilla Pomeroy came to me the other night with the information that her husband was the Senator's murderer; then, the next morning, Mrs. Rhodes gave me some exclusive information about the common-law marriage of Mr. Rhodes some years ago . . . you probably read all about it in my *Globe* piece."

"And wondered where you'd got it, too. What did Mrs. Pomeroy tell you exactly?"

I repeated her warnings, omitting our tender dalliance as irrelevant.

"I don't understand," sighed Winters.

"The only thought which occurs to me is that they are *both* beneficiaries. I've thought all along that we should be real old-fashioned and examine the relations of the three beneficiaries of the late Senator." I had not of course thought of this until now; it seemed suddenly significant, though.

"We do that continually," said Winters.

"It's possible one of them killed him for the inheritance."

"Quite possible."

"On the other hand, he might have been killed for political reasons."

"Also possible."

"Then again he might have been killed for reasons of revenge."

"Very likely."

"In other words, Lieutenant Winters, you haven't the foggiest notion why he was killed or who killed him."

"That's very blunt, but that's about it." Winters seemed not at all disturbed.

I had a sudden suspicion. "You wouldn't by any chance be thinking of allowing this case to go unsolved, would you? Stopping it right here, with a confession and a corpse who, presumably, made the confession before committing suicide."

"Whatever made you think that?" said Winters blandly, and I knew then that that was exactly what he had in mind. I couldn't blame him: by admitting that Hollister had been killed and the confession faked, he put himself squarely behind the eight-ball, a position which the servants of the public like even less than we civilians do. Though he might have proven to all and sundry that he was a pretty sharp character to guess that Hollister was killed, he would also be running the risk of never finding the murderer, which would mean that public confidence in the police would be shaken, in which event he himself would be shaken back to a beat in Georgetown. I could hardly blame him for this indifference to the true cause of justice. After all, who really cared if the Senator and Hollister had been murdered? No one mourned the passage of either to the grave. For a moment love of law and sense of right wavered, but then I recalled myself to stern duty (the fact that I would have the success of the year if I could unearth the murderer after the case had been nominally shut by the police affected my right action somewhat).

"How long will you hold the crew together?" I asked, writing Winters off as an ally.

"Another day or so, until all the evidence is double-checked . . . the autopsy and so on completed."

"We will then be free to go?"

"Unless something unforeseen happens."

"Like another murder?"

"There won't be another murder," he said confidently, and I wondered if he might have some evidence which I didn't have. After all, it was just possible that Hollister *had* committed suicide . . . driven to it by Mr. X, the possessor of the documents, a whimsical cuss who was obviously enjoying himself immensely.

"What about the gun?"

"Well, what about it? It belonged to Mrs. Rhodes, didn't it?"

"That's right . . . no prints on it except Hollister's. Mrs. Rhodes kept the gun in the table beside her bed. She hadn't looked at it in over a month. Anyone could have gone in there and taken it."

"But how many people in the house would have known there was a gun in that night-table?"

"I haven't any idea. Hollister knew, though." He smiled contentedly. "He knew where everything was."

"Except the papers which the Senator had hidden in the study, which someone else found first."

"But who?"

"The murderer."

"I see no evidence."

"The evidence is in front of you, or rather in the other room being gone over by your lawyer. How does this Mr. X know so much about the case? How did he know where to find the papers? Why did he send them to me at all since Hollister's death was intended to finish the case?"

"It may be," said Lieutenant Winters in the voice of innumerable Mary Roberts Rinehart heroines, "that we shall never know."

"Go to hell," I said.

He frowned. "Why don't you stop fussing around, Sargeant? This is none of your business, we all have a perfect out. Let's take it. I am as dedicated to duty as anyone, and I don't intend to drop the case, really; but I'm not going to beat my brains out over it and I *am* going to pretend it's all finished. I suggest you do the same." This was a threat, nicely phrased.

"I will," I said. "But I'm not going to let it go unsolved if I can help it." We sat staring hostilely at one another . . . conscious of the righteousness of my tone, I was almost ready to recite the Wet Nurses' Creed in a voice choked with emotion. But I let it ride.

"Well, I better be going," I said, standing up.

"Thanks for letting me have the papers."

"Think nothing of it." Full of wrath, I departed.

3

Mrs. Goldmountain lived in a large house of yellow stone, mellowed with age, in Georgetown, the ancient part of the city where, in re-made slums of Federal vintage, the more fashionable Washingtonians dwell. Her house, however, was larger than all the others, the former residence of some historic personage.

I was shown to an upstairs sitting-room, hung in yellow silk, all very Directoire. After a moment's wait, Mrs. Goldmountain appeared, neat in black and hung with diamonds. "Mr. Sargeant, isn't this nice? I was so happy you could come to the party last night with darling Ellen . . . poor shattered lamb!" I could see now why I had been admitted so quickly, without hesitation: I was straight from the Senator's house and would know, presumably, all about the murders. I had every intention of indulging La Goldmountain.

"She's taking it very well," I said, which was putting it as nicely as possible.

"She was devoted to Lee Rhodes. Of course they never saw much of each other, but everyone knew of their devotion. They were so alike."

I failed to see any resemblance, but that was beside

the point. I mumbled something about "like father like daughter".

"Of course some people were shocked by her going out so soon after his death, but *I* said, after all she is young and high-spirited and there is nothing, simply nothing she can do about his being dead. I love tradition, you know, but I see no reason for being a slave to it, do you? Of course not. They must all be relieved that that horrible man who killed himself confessed."

"Yes, we were pretty happy about that: I mean, justice being done and all that."

"Of course. Is it true that poor Roger Pomeroy was nearly arrested?"

I said that it was true.

"How frightful if the wrong man had been convicted! I have always liked Roger Pomeroy, not that our paths have crossed very often, just official places, that's all, especially during the war when he was here on one of those committees. I never took to *her*, I'm afraid; I always thought her rather common, never having the *slightest* notion that she was really Lee's daughter, like *that!* What a cross it must have been for her to bear: it could explain everything. My analyst, who studied with Dr. Freud in Vienna, always said that whatever happens to you in the first nine months before you're born determines everything. Well, I mean if the poor little thing *knew* before she was born that she was illegitimate (and they've practically proven that we *do* know such things . . . we later forget them during the trauma of birth, like amnesia) it would certainly have given her a complex and explained why I always thought her just a little bit common."

I stopped the flow gradually. I diffidently explained my proposition to her.

"For some time now my clients, the Heigh-Ho Dog-food Company, have wanted an outstanding public relations campaign. I've tried any number of ideas on them, but none was exactly right. The campaign we had in mind must have dignity as well as public appeal, and, you will admit, those two things aren't easy to find together. The long and the short of it, Mrs. Goldmountain, is that I think we could make a dandy campaign out of Hermione."

"Oh, but I could never consent . . ." she began, but I knew my Goldmountain.

"We would arrange . . . Heigh-Ho would arrange . . . for her to give a recital at Town Hall. As a result of all that publicity she would appear on television, on radio and perhaps even a movie contract might be forthcoming. You, as her owner, would of course lend considerable dignity to all of this, and though the publicity might be distasteful . . ."

That did it. Any mention of publicity made Mrs. Goldmountain vibrate with lust.

"If I were to accept such a proposal, I would insist on supervising Hermione's activities myself."

"I think that is a fair request . . . I'm sure Heigh-Ho would consult you on everything."

"I would also insist on having final say about her programme at Town Hall. I know what her capacities are, and I know the things she can do. I would never permit her to sing any of these modern songs, only the classics and of course the National Anthem."

"You will be allowed to choose the repertoire of course. Also the voice coach."

"You feel she *needs* a coach?" I had made a blunder.

"All the stars at the Metropolitan have voice coaches," I said quickly. "To keep their voices limbered up."

"In that case, I would be advised by you," said Mrs. Goldmountain graciously, her eyes narrowing as she saw the spread in *Life* as well as the image of Hermione and herself flickering greyly on the little screen in millions of homes.

"What songs does she do best?" I asked, closing in.

"German *Lieder,* and Italian opera. If you like we can hear her now."

"Oh no," I said quickly, "not now, some other time. I know her genius already. All Washington does, and, soon, the whole world will know."

"You may tell Heigh-Ho, that I shall seriously entertain any offer they wish to make." And so our treaty was fashioned. I asked permission to telephone the Vice-President of Heigh-Ho in New York. It was granted. The official was delighted with my plan and made an appointment to meet Mrs. Goldmountain the next morning, in Washington.

Everyone was happy and my firm was again on solid footing. Mrs. Goldmountain invited me to take tea with her and a few guests who were at this moment arriving. One of them turned out to be the new Senator, former Governor Johnson Ledbetter.

"Remember you well!" he boomed, pumping my hand. "A much less unhappy occasion I am glad to say." He beamed vaguely and accepted a drink from the butler. I took tea, as did our hostess and the two other guests; one a political commentator of great seriousness, the other Elmer Bush, who had arrived while I was greeting the Senator. Elmer was every bit as cordial as the old political ham, both slices off the same haunch, as it were.

"Well, it looks like you're all innocent," said Elmer toothily as we stepped back out of the main line of chatter which circulated around the new Senator and Mrs. Goldmountain.

"It certainly does, Elmer."

"I suppose you'll be going back to New York?"

"Very soon."

"Winters, I gather, is very pleased about the way the case shaped up, very pleased."

"I should think so."

"Quite a trick of his, pretending to arrest Pomeroy while really making a trap for Hollister."

"Trap?"

"Isn't that what happened? Wasn't Hollister driven to commit suicide by the police? Naturally, they wouldn't admit anything like that but it *seems* clear: they pretended to have evidence which they didn't have, forced him to confess and then to kill himself, an ingenious, a masterful display of policemanship."

Elmer Bush never joked so I assumed that he was serious and left him rigorously alone.

"I've already discussed it on my show. You probably saw it night before last, got a good response too. The public seems unusually interested in this affair, something out of the ordinary, Senator being murdered and all that, very different. I thought I might drop by and take a few shots of the house on film to be used in my next programme . . ." And he tantalised me with promises of glory if I would help him get in to see the house and Mrs. Rhodes. I told him I would do what I could.

Across the room the Senator-designate was booming.

"Dear lady, I will be saddened indeed if you don't attend the swearing in tomorrow at the Capitol. The Vice-President is going to do it, in his office, just a few friends will be there, very cosy, and the press. Say the word, and I shall have my secretary send you a ticket."

"It will be a moment to be cherished," said our hostess, looking up into his full-blown face, like a gardener examining a favourite rose for beetles.

"I am only saddened that my appearance in the halls of

Congress should have been like this . . . in the place of an old and treasured friend. How tragical!"

A murmur of sympathy eddied about him. "Lee was a man to be remembered," said the statesman.

His oration was shorter than I had suspected; when it was over he and Elmer Bush fell into conversation about the coming convention while I chatted with Mrs. Goldmountain.

"You're going to be in Washington a little while longer?"

"Two days at least . . . so the police say."

"Why on earth do they want you now that it's all over?"

"Red tape. You know how they are."

"Well, give my love to darling Ellen and tell her to come see me before she goes back."

"I certainly will."

"'And also to Mrs. Rhodes." She paused and sipped some tea, her black eyes dreamy. "She must be relieved."

"That the case is finally over?"

"In *every* sense," said Mrs. Goldmountain significantly.

"What do you mean?"

"Only what everyone in Washington knows and has always known, that she hated Lee Rhodes, that she tried, on least two occasions, to divorce him and that he somehow managed to talk her out of it. I'm quite sure it was a relief to her when he was killed, by someone else. That awful Hollister really *did* do it, didn't he?"

4

I returned to the house shortly after five, and went straight to my room. As I bathed and dressed for dinner, I had a vague feeling that a pattern was beginning to evolve but precisely what I could not tell. It was definite that there

139

were a number of charades being performed by a number of people for a number of reasons . . . figure out the meaning of the charades and the identity of the murderer would become clear.

I combed my hair and began to construct a plan of attack. First, the Pomeroys. It was necessary that I discover what her game was, why she had come to me with that story about her husband. I should also find out why he had been, all in all, so calm about his arrest: had he been so sure of vindication? And, if he had, why?

Second, I should like to investigate Mrs. Rhodes's whole mysterious performance, her reference to the paper-chase, her possible authorship of the anonymous letters, the fact of her revolver's use as a murder weapon. What had her relationship been, truly, to Senator Rhodes? I found Mrs. Goldmountain's assertion difficult to believe. Yet she had, heaven knew, no reason to be dishonest and if Mrs. Rhodes *had* detested her husband. . . . I thought of that firm old mouth, the controlled voice and gestures: I could imagine her quite easily killing her husband. But how could I find out? Ellen was much too casual about her family to know. Verbena Pruitt seemed the likeliest source, the old family friend . . . except it would not be easy to get anything out of her; she was too used to the world of politics, of secrecy and deals to be caught in an indiscretion. Still I decided to give her a try that evening.

The third charade concerned my erstwhile ally Lieutenant Winters. As a matter of curiosity I wanted to know just what game *he* was playing, what was the reason for his apparent desertion of the case.

And, finally, there was always Langdon; the idea that he might have committed a political murder appealed to me enormously: it was all very romantic and Graustarkian . . . unfortunately he hardly seemed the type to do in poor

Hollister, but then murder knoweth no type as the detectives' Hand Manual would say, if there was such a thing.

Verbena Pruitt could undoubtedly have done the murders, but there was no motive as far as I could tell. Ellen was quite capable of murdering her father, me, Langdon and the President of the United States, but she had been at the Chevy Chase Club when Hollister was murdered, as had Langdon, ruling them both out.

This left Verbena Pruitt and Mrs. Rhodes as the only two who were in the house at the time of Hollister's death (the Pomeroys had been at the police station). The murderer then, barring the intervention of an outsider, was either Verbena or Mrs. Rhodes and, of the two, only Mrs. Rhodes had had the motive.

The result of all this deductive reasoning left me a little cold. I sat down heavily on the bed, hair-brush in hand and wondered why I hadn't worked all this out before. My next thought concerned Winters. He had obviously worked it out for himself. He must've known for some hours what the situation was; he had studied all the statements, had known where each of us was. He must know then that Mrs. Rhodes was, very likely, the murderer and yet he had seemed ready to give up the case. Why? Had he been bought off? This was altogether too possible, knowing the ways of the police, in my own city of New York anyway. Or had he, out of a sense of chivalry, not chosen to arrest her, preferring to rest on the laurels provided him by Hollister's apparent suicide?

I began to think that it might be a good idea if I forgot about the whole thing. I had no desire to see justice done, either in the abstract or in this particular case. Let the tyrants go to their graves unavenged, such was my poetical thought.

The telephone by my bed rang. I answered it. Ellen was on the line. "Come to my room like a good boy," she commanded. "We can have a drink before dinner."

She was already dressed for dinner when I opened the door; she was buffing her nails at her dressing-table. "There's a drink over there on the table, by the bed." And sure enough there was a Martini waiting for me. I saluted her and drank; then I sat in a chintzy chair, looking at her. I have always enjoyed watching women make themselves up, the one occupation to which they bring utter sincerity and complete dedication. Ellen was no exception.

"When are you going back?" she asked, examining her nails in the light, a critical, distracted expression on her face.

"I hope tomorrow," I said. "It depends on Winters."

"I'm going to go tomorrow, too," she said flatly. "I'm tired of all this. I'm sick of the reporters and the police, even though that Winters is something of a dear . . . and on top of all that I have, ever since I can remember, loathed Washington. I wonder if we could get out of here to-night?" She put down her piece of chamois, or whatever it was she was polishing her nails with, and looked at me.

"I doubt it," I said. "For one thing Winters will be here."

"Oh damn!"

"And for another thing I don't think those detectives would let us go without permission from him."

"We could duck them; there's a side door off the small drawing-room nobody ever uses. We could get out there; there's no guard on that side of the house. . . " As she spoke she sounded, for the first time since I'd known her, nervous and upset.

"Why do you want to leave so badly?"

"Peter, I'm scared to death." And she was, too; her face was drawn beneath the skilful make-up and her hands shook as she drank her Martini.

"Why? There's nothing to be afraid of, is there?"

"I. . . ." Then she stopped, as though changing her mind about something. "Peter, let's go back tonight, after Winters leaves."

"It wouldn't look right; on top of that we might be in contempt of court or something." I was very curious, but it was up to her to tell me why she wanted, so suddenly, to get out of Washington.

She lit her cigarette with that abrupt masculine gesture of hers, quite unlike any other girls I had known. This seemed to soothe her. "I suppose I'm just getting jittery, that's all, delayed reaction."

"I *will* say you've been unnaturally calm through everything; in fact I've never seen anything like the way you and your mother both managed to be so clear-headed and unemotional about everything." This was a direct shot and it hit home; a flicker of emotion went across her face, like a bird's shadow in the sun. But she told me nothing.

"We're a cold-blooded family, I guess."

"I can understand *you*," I said. "I mean you'd lived away from home so long and you didn't care much about your father, but Mrs. Rhodes . . . well, it's quite something the way she's taken all this."

"Ah," said Ellen distractedly. She stood up. "I think I'll go mix us another Martini. I keep the stuff in the bathroom . . . force of habit. In the old days I always had a mouthwash bottle full of gin." She disappeared. I stood up and stretched. I could hear Ellen rattling around in the bathroom . . . . somewhere in the house a door slammed, a toilet was flushed: life went on, regardless of crisis. In a pleasantly elegiac mood, brought on by the first Martini and increased by the knowledge that soon there would be a second, I wandered about the room, examining the girlhood books of my one-time fiancée. It was an odd group. The

Bobbsie Twins were next to *Fanny Hill* and *Lady Chatterley* nestled the *Rover Boys,* as she might well have done in life. It was obvious that Ellen's girlhood interests had changed abruptly with puberty. Only a bound volume of the *Congressional Record* attested to her birth and position in life, and *it* looked unopened.

"Here you are, love." She looked somewhat rosier and I decided that she had very likely had herself a large dividend, if not a capital gain, while she was preparing my drink. I toasted her again and we discussed the merits of *Fanny Hill* until dinner-time.

For the first time since I had arrived in Washington nearly a week before, the company at table could have been described as hearty. It was not clever nor amusing, the guests were too solid for that, but it was at least not gloomy and everyone drank Burgundy with the roast and even Mrs. Rhodes smiled over her black lace and jet, like the moon in its last quarter.

I watched her carefully for some sign of guilt, some bloody ensign like Lady Macbeth's spotted hand, but she was as serene as ever, and if she was a murderess she wore her crimes with an easy air.

I sat beside Roger Pomeroy and we talked to one another for the first time in some days; he was most cheery. "Had a most profitable visit with the Defence Department today," he said, drying his lips after a mouthful of wine, staining the napkin dark red . . . I was full of blood-images that night.

"About your new explosive?"

"That's right. I gather it's been checked out favourably by their engineers and chemists and it looks as though they'll be placing an order with us soon."

"All this *without* the Senator's help?"

Pomeroy smiled grimly. "There's a new Senator . . . as

of tomorrow anyway. We made it very clear that Talisman City was a pretty important place come next November and that the Administration would do well to keep us happy."

"And it worked?"

"Seems to've. Tomorrow Cam and I are flying back home. I'll be glad to get out of this god-damned town, you may be sure."

"Do you think they'd really have been able to convict you?" It was the first time I had ever mentioned the murder directly to him, out of sympathy for a 'murderer's' feelings.

"Hell no!" He set his glass down with a thump. "In the first place that young fool Winters went off half-cocked. He assumed that since the explosive was mine and I was angry at Lee for his behaviour about the new contract and I knew that my wife stood to inherit a lot of money, that I went ahead and killed him. How dumb can you get? I was perfectly willing to kill Lee if I'd thought I could get away with it. But not in his own house and under suspicious circumstances; besides, in business you never kill anybody, as much as you'd like to." He chuckled.

"Even so, they felt they had enough evidence to convict you with."

"All circumstantial . . . every last bit of it."

"How did you plan to get out of it, though? A lot of people have been ruined on much less evidence than Winters had on you.'

"Oh, I had a way." He grinned craftily. He was a little tight and in an expansive mood.

"An alibi?"

"In a way." He paused. "Now this is in absolute confidence . . . if you repeat it I'll call you a liar." He beamed at me, full of self-esteem. "I didn't need Lee. Before I even got to Washington I had contacted someone else, someone very highly placed who promised to help me get the contract. That person was able to do it . . . had, in fact, told me that the contract would be forthcoming in the next ten days, told me in a letter sent the day before Lee was killed, special delivery, too, which I am pleased to say would have proven that I knew before I talked to Lee that the contract was set."

"Why did you talk to him then?"

Pomeroy frowned. "Because Lee and I had been involved in a number of other deals before we quarrelled. He was a vindictive man, like a devil when he thought that he was right about something, or rather that something was right for *him* . . . a bit of a difference, if you get what I mean. He was the boss of the state and it's a good idea to clear anything which has to do with patronage and government contracts with the boss . . . that's a simple rule of politics."

"Then you had to have his O.K.?"

"No, but it would have helped. I was angry with him but that was all. I was a long way from being the 'desperate and ruined man' which the papers and the police thought I was."

"Why didn't you tell the police right off that you had already got the contract and that consequently there was no real motive for killing Lee Rhodes?"

Pomeroy smiled at me pityingly, as though unaware anyone could have reached the age of twenty-nine in a state of ignorance of business and politics comparable to my own. He spoke slowly, as though to a child. "If I had told the police that I had already fixed the contract, they would have asked for proof. I would have had to show them the letter. They would have got in touch with the author of the letter who would have been embarrassed and possibly ruined by the publicity. This country is run on one set of principles while pretending to another. Contracts are *supposed* to go to the best and the most economical company. Pomeroy Inc. is a perfectly good company but so are a hundred others; to get a contract I must use influence . . . if I had exposed my benefactor I would have lost the contract, the friendship of a powerful person, my business . . ."

"But you would have saved your life."

"My life was never in any danger. If things had got bad I would have told the whole story but I knew damn well they wouldn't be able to indict me . . . though I suppose they came pretty close."

One thing still bothered me. "Why did you and the Senator fall out in the first place? Why wouldn't he back you up with the Defence Department?"

Pomeroy chuckled. "Lee always got the best price possible for his services. I was outbid, after ten years. A rival company bought him and he stayed bought, like they say. A big outfit from the North which has been expanding all over the country started up in Talisman City a year ago and since they're real professionals they went to Lee right off and underwrote his campaign for the nomination. You probably know who I mean if you were handling his publicity."

"I knew indeed . . . one of the biggest cartels in the country. I had known they were contributors; I had no idea they were buyers as well.

"There wasn't much I could do against them. Lee wanted to help me, you know, but he couldn't. At least not until after the nominating convention was over, by which time I'd have been out of business. So I managed the deal without him. I only came to see him to find out about the future, to find out how long they had him tied up. I never *did* find that out. Lee was a devil, never think he wasn't. He was cold and shrewd and he would've sacrificed his own mother for his career. He didn't care about anybody except my wife. I don't know why, but Cam and he were awfully close and he liked her better than Ellen, better than his wife, too. If only because of that, we could've proven that I'd not've been likely to kill him . . . in spite of the inheritance. He never liked me much but he would never have hurt her if he could have helped it. In time he would've made it up to us. I'm sure of that. Anyway, I was never in much danger."

The pieces fell gradually into place. It was like a jigsaw puzzle. I was now at the point where I had filled in the sky, got the frame of the picture all put together: now all that I had to do was fit the central pieces in, numerous tiny pieces, many of them the colour of blood.

Winters had attended the dinner but not once did he speak to me or look in my direction. He spoke mostly to Camilla Pomeroy and Walter Langdon. After dinner we went into the drawing-room. By the time I was seated, coffee in hand, the minion of the law had disappeared. His departure was noticed by no one, as far as I could tell.

I tried to manoeuvre towards Mrs. Rhodes but she, as though divining my plot, excused herself and went off to bed.

Langdon and Ellen played backgammon at the far end of the room; I noticed they no longer seemed to enjoy one another's company as much as formerly, and it looked as though Ellen would soon be in the market again for another fiancé. This shouldn't be difficult, I thought, recalling that not only was she a handsome uninhibited piece but that she was now worth close to a million dollars, before taxes.

The Pomeroys conversed contentedly by the fire and

Verbena Pruitt and I, the couple left over, fell into conversation.

"You have had quite an introduction to Washington," said the lady of state, her face creasing amiably.

"It's not what I'd expected."

"I should think not. It's lucky for all of us that everything worked out as neatly as it did. It could've been one of those cases where nothing was ever proved and everyone would have remained under suspicion for years . . . and that, young man, is *grist* for political enemies."

"Grist," I repeated sagely.

"Rufus didn't use his head," said Miss Pruitt thoughtfully, fondling a cluster of wax red cherries which a malicious dress-designer had sewed in strategic places to her coffee-coloured gown. "If I'd been he I wouldn't have given up that easy. Suppose those papers *had* come to light and he *was* involved in a business scandal . . . who could have proven that he killed Lee? The worst that would've happened was a jail sentence for larceny, or whatever the crime was. Besides, how did he know that all this was going to come to light, anyway?"

"I suppose that someone had threatened to expose him . . . someone who knew about the plot, the business deals, and also knew about the murder . . ." Miss Pruitt had obviously thought about this more carefully than one might have suspected.

"Piffle!" said Miss Pruitt in a voice which made the others start. Then, lowering her voice and looking at me significantly, she said: "Why would anyone want to do that?"

"Revenge?"

"Not very likely . . . to avenge Lee? Perhaps, but it seems far-fetched."

"On the other hand, assuming Hollister was murdered by

149

the Senator's murderer, that would make no sense either since Pomeroy was obviously going to be indicted for the murder, and since *he* was to take the rap there was hardly any reason to confuse matters further by killing Hollister and making *him* seem like the murderer."

"I have not of course allowed myself to think that Rufus was killed. Yet, if he had been it might've been by someone who wanted to get Pomeroy off."

"The only two people who were interested in that were both at the police station when Rufus was shot."

"Who can tell?" said Miss Pruitt mysteriously, detaching a wax cherry by mistake; she looked at it unhappily for a moment; then she plunged it between her melonish breasts.

"It could be," I said, trying to divert my morbid attention from her well-packed bodice, "that we are being much too subtle about all this. Hollister might have been remorseful; he might have known that his business dealings were going to be found out anyway, and he might've thought: what the hell, I'm going to jail anyway. I might as well confess, save Pomeroy and get out of this mess 'with a bare bodkin'."

"'For who would fardels bear. . . .'" boomed Miss Pruitt, recognising my allusion to him who they call 'the bard' in political circles. She fardeled on for a moment or two; then, her soliloquy done: "It's possible you're right," she said. "Since it is the police view, I am perfectly willing to subscribe to it. I will follow them down the line *one hundred* per cent."

It took me several moments to get her off the subject of Rufus Hollister and on to Mrs. Rhodes. The closer I got to what interested me, though, the more reticent the stateswoman became.

"Yes, she is taking all this bravely, isn't she? Of course

she has character. Women of our generation do have character, though I am some years younger than she. Of course, living with Lee was not the easiest experience. He was a difficult man; that type is. I think to be the wife of a politician is the worst fate in the world, and I should know because I'm both a woman *and* a politician."

"But they were fond of each other?"

She paused just long enough to confirm my suspicions. "They were very close," she said, without conviction.

"Did she have much to do with his official life . . . elections and all that?"

"Not much. She handled the finances, though. I believe they owned everything jointly. I think she wanted him to retire this year. but then all political wives are the same: she opposed his going after the nomination, which was good sense because he had no chance of getting it." She looked craftily into the middle distance, implying that she knew who would be the peerless standard-bearer.

"Would you say that she had a vindictive nature?"

If I had slapped the great woman, I could not've got a more startled reaction. "What makes you ask that?" she blustered.

"Oh, I don't know. It had occurred to me that she might have been the one who threatened Rufus, forced him to confess."

"Nonsense!" Alarm rippled through the Pruitt, like a revolution in an African ant-hill; her face turned dark and I was afraid she might have a stroke; but then the odd convulsions ceased and she added quietly: "Charity could be her middle name. Her life has been one long martyrdom, endured without complaint. She hated politics; she hated the idea of Camilla Pomeroy . . . as well she might; she almost died when Ellen ran off with a gymnast and the marriage had to be annulled . . ."

"I thought she married him in a church, properly." I recalled the photograph of Ellen in wedding veil which the Senator kept in his study.

"No, she was supposed to marry an eligible young man, a fine upstanding lad who might have made something out of her. Two days before the wedding, a wedding which her parents approved of, even though she was only seventeen, she ran off with this muscular animal. Her father caught her in Elkton, Maryland, and the marriage was duly annulled. Yet in spite of the scandal, her mother took her back without a reproach. Her father . . ." The butler crept into the room to inform Miss Pruitt that there was a telephone call for her.

She disappeared into the hall. I sat drowsily by the fire. A moment later, she appeared, very pale, and asked me for brandy. I got some for her.

She gulped it sloppily, spilling half of it on her majestic front. I looked about the room to see if the others had noticed anything; they had not; they were deep in their own problems.

"Has anything happened?" I asked.

She dabbed at her dress with a piece of Kleenex; she was, for her, pale . . . her face mottled pink-grey. "That was Governor Ledbetter. It seems that the papers have got hold of some business deal he and Lee were involved in; something which involved Rufus: the thing he referred to in that confession. A terrible scandal. . . ."

SIX

I

"MORAL turpitude," said the Senate, and they refused to seat the Senator-designate until a committee had checked him out.

The morning was full of meetings and reports in the house. Mrs. Rhodes and Miss Pruitt were especially upset. Langdon was remarkably interested (at last having found a suitable theme for his magazine), and even the Pomeroys delayed their trip back to Talisman City to find out what would happen. To what extent Pomeroy himself was involved in the Senator's numerous deals, I did not know. As far as I could tell, not at all: in this one at least.

After breakfast, I conferred with Winters, who, under the ruse of taking some last photographs of the Senator's study and of Rufus Hollister's bedroom, had returned to the house where he was largely ignored, in marked contrast to his earlier visits.

I found him alone in the study. The wall which had been blown away was now repaired, as far as the brick went. The plastering had not been done, however, so the room had a raw look to it: half panelled and half new-laid brick.

Winters was glancing idly at some of the scrap-books when I came in.

"Oh, it's you." He sounded neutral, to say the least. He looked calmer and happier than usual . . . with good reason, considering that he was now off the hot seat, his case successfully concluded.

"Did you ever go through these?" I asked, looking over his shoulder at a yellowed clipping, dated 1927: a photograph of the Senator shaking hands with a slim woman in a cloche hat.

"Oh yes."

I tried to read the caption of the picture, Winters tried to turn the page; I deliberately lifted his hand off the page and read the caption: "Senator Rhodes being congratulated on his recent victory in the primaries by Verbena Pruitt, National Committeewoman."

"Who would've thought she ever looked like that?" I was impressed. It was impossible to tell what her face was like in this old picture . . . but she had had a good figure.

"I don't think she was ever much," said Winters; if he was irritated with the abrupt way I had pushed him aside, he didn't show it.

"What do you think about this new development?"

"What new development?" He looked at me blandly.

"You know what I mean. This business which Hollister was to take the rap for, it's come out in the papers."

"The case is finished," said Winters, opening the 1936 scrap-book.

"Who got the word to the papers?"

"I haven't any idea."

"According to the *Times,* the Government has been investigating the Senator's company for two years."

"I think that's right." Winters sounded bored.

"According to the papers this morning, the Senator was just as much implicated as Hollister."

"Yes?"

"In other words, it doesn't look as if Hollister was to

have taken the rap for the Senator's misdeeds . . . in other words, the confession was a phony."

"Very logical," said Winters, admiring a Berryman cartoon of Lee Rhodes in the *Washington Star.*

"I'll say it's logical." I was growing irritated. "Is there any real evidence that Hollister was to take the rap for the Governor and Rhodes? According to the newspaper account, they were all in it equally."

"What about the papers you got in the mail from your anonymous admirer? What about them? They proved that the Senator had fixed it for Hollister to be the front man. Hollister killed him before he could finish the arrangements . . . that's simple enough, isn't it?"

"You don't really believe that?"

"Why not?" And that was the most that I could get out of Winters. The thought that someone might have bought *him* occurred to me again with some force. More than ever was I determined to meddle in this affair.

While he looked at the old clippings, I wandered about the study, looking at the bomb-scarred desk, the books on the shelves. Then, aware that I was going to get no satisfaction out of Winters, I left the study, without a word of farewell. I had about twenty-four hours, I knew, in which to produce the murderer, and since I had almost nothing to go on, it was a little difficult to determine what to do next. I had several ideas, none very good.

It occurred to me, being of a logical disposition, that I might come to a solution more quickly than not if I were to proceed in an orderly way to examine each of the suspects and then, by collating their stories, arrive at a solution. It sounded remarkably easy; in fact, just the thought of being logical so delighted me that for several minutes I enjoyed the sensation of having solved the murder successfully.

I had taken care of Pomeroy. I knew, very likely, more

about his relations with the Senator than the police did, thanks to Mrs. Rhodes's excellent Burgundy of the night before.

I still had certain doubts about Camilla. She was the next logical person to eliminate. Why, I wondered, had she tried to make me think her husband was the murderer? It was an important point, all the more so since she was a beneficiary in the old man's will, and had known it, too.

I found her off by herself in a corner of the drawing-room, studying the latest issue of *Harper's Bazaar*. She was reading the thin ribbon of text which accompanies the advertisements; this thin ribbon was, I could see, the work of the latest young novelist: it concerned a young boy in Montgomery, Alabama, who killed nine flies in as many minutes on the eve of the Fourth of July . . . I had read it earlier, being of a literary turn (though I belong to the older literary generation of Carson McCullers and have never quite absorbed the newcomers, even though they take mighty nice photographs).

"I just love it," said Camilla, without enthusiasm, closing the magazine; she was dressed in a very business-like suit, as though ready for travelling.

"We were going to take the noon train, Roger and I, but since poor Johnson got involved in this terrible mess, Roger thought, out of loyalty, we should stay and see him through."

"I think that's swell," I said earnestly.

"Yes," she said brightly. We stood looking at one another awkwardly for perhaps a minute. Even in this age of jet planes and chromium plate, there are certain proprieties which those who occupy the upper echelon of our society insist upon maintaining, regardless of their true feelings. It is usually agreed upon in these circles that when a man has gone to bed with a gentlewoman he has become, up to a point, her *cavaliere servente,* as they used to say in Venice . . . the Venetians used to say, that is.

It was apparent to both of us that a certain dignity was lacking in our relationship; neither had spoken of love or duty, and both, in fact, had acted subsequently as though nothing had happened, depriving man's greatest emotion and most sacred moment of its true splendour; in fact, there had been the faintest note of the barnyard in our coupling which, doubtless, worried the hen, though the rooster, if I can call myself one even in this analogy, was not much concerned. But there was a game to be played . . . two games, even . . . and I had very little time.

"Camilla," the name sounded rich and husky on my lips.

"Yes?" Her voice squeaked just a little as she turned two dark bright eyes up at me.

"I . . . I wonder if you'd have lunch with me."

"Oh, but . . ." She 'butted' for a few moments, and then, aware that her position as a lady was at stake, she agreed to a brief lunch at the Mayflower, where the food was good in the cocktail lounge and there was a string quartette.

The Mayflower was very grand; I had been there only once before, in the main dining-room. This time we went to the cocktail lounge, a dim, marbleised, ferny place full of people dining in the gloom to the sound of soft music; it was a perfect place for an assignation. Unfortunately the customers were mainly ladies who had dropped in after a hard morning of shopping, or five-percenters discussing deals with prospective clients . . . the Congressional and political figures did not, presumably, lunch here, though they could be found, often, in this room at five o'clock.

We were led to a corner table by a distinguish-looking

157

head waiter who resembled a Bavarian Foreign Minister.

"Here we are," said Camilla, and a high mouse giggle escaped from behind her ruddy lips; she was very nervous. I could not imagine that this great plain fool was the same woman who had only a few nights before come to my room like a winged furnace, like Lady Potiphar at the end of the first month. Dressed and full of rectitude, she seemed what she was: an ordinary girl from Talisman City.

We ordered cold Virginia ham and mint juleps. I have always hated mint juleps, and I don't think she cared for them either, but somehow our proximity to the Old Dominion made us reckless; outside, snow was wetly falling.

"I suppose you look forward to getting back home?" I began formally.

"I certainly look forward to leaving this horrid city," she said sincerely, biting off a piece of mint.

"It hasn't been a very nice time for any of us," I said.

"We have aged, Roger and I, a hundred years," she said, looking deep into my eyes. Unfortunately the stately gloom of the place prevented me from experiencing the full power of those shining dark eyes.

"It looks as though his contract is all set, doesn't it?"

She nodded. "I'm told the first orders are being made up now. We couldn't be more thrilled."

"I should think so. Do you think you'll start back to-night?"

She shook her head. "No, not now. Of course it may not be as nice as I think."

"What may not be?"

"Home. My friends. What on earth will they think when they know? And of course they know now; *everyone* does."

"Knows what?"

"That I am Lee's daughter. I hardly dare face them at the club, assuming we'll be allowed to keep our membership." We were approaching by a circuitous route the true soul of Camilla Pomeroy: the club and all that the club meant.

"At least your mother was his common-law wife." This didn't sound too good, but my intention was kindly.

"As if that will make any difference to *them*. No, I must face this thing through." She set her jaw, a sprig of mint clenched between her teeth.

"It's hardly your fault, your birth."

"You don't understand Talisman City," she said grimly. "The people there live by the book . . ."

"And have not charity . . ."

"What?"

"And are difficult," I said. I have always regarded as a stroke of good fortune that I was not born or brought up in a small American town; they may be the backbone of the nation, but they are also the backbone of ignorance, bigotry, and boredom, all in vast quantities. I remember one brief stay in a little up-state New York village where I was referred to, behind my back, as 'the Jew from New York City', despite the presence of a Sargeant at that very moment in the Episcopal Council of Bishops . . . such is the generous feeling of our American peasants for strangers; I didn't envy Mrs. Pomeroy's return to her native heath.

"Oh, very. But then we *have* to have standards after all," she said, showing she was one of them, fallen or not.

While we lunched, we talked about her early days, about the Senator. "We were very close, even though I never dreamed the truth. Mother would never say anything except that she was glad I was seeing him because he was such a distinguished man. She was especially pleased when

I organised a platoon of Girl Scouts to work for him on one of his campaigns. Father, that is her husband, hated Lee, and used to make very uncivil remarks whenever I came home from one of my visits to the Rhodes' house, but Mother always made him keep still."

"It must've been quite a shock, when you found out."

She rolled her eyes briefly to heaven. "I'll say it was. I thought seriously of killing myself, being young and dramatic, but then after a while I got used to the idea . . . and Lee was marvellous with me, called me 'his own girl'."

She seemed, suddenly, very moved, for the first time since the trouble began.

"He must have been very fond of you. He would have to have been to include you in his will, knowing everything would come to light, embarrassing his family."

"Much he cared about them!" This came out like a small explosion.

"You mean . . ."

"He hated both of them. Mrs. Rhodes was an ice-cold woman who married him because he was a young man who was going to make his mark, because *she* was ambitious. He went into politics and ruined his health and got mixed up with all sorts of terrible people and finally was killed by one of them just because she wanted to be a Senator's wife, a President's wife. How he used to complain to me about her! And his daughter: well, he understood her altogether too well . . . everyone did, what she was and is. Of course, he stopped her that once, when she ran off with a weight-lifter on the eve of her wedding to Verbena Pruitt's nephew . . ."

"She was supposed to marry Verbena's nephew?" I had not heard this before.

"That was the plan, only at the last minute, after the wedding dress was made and the reception already planned,

160

she left home with this man. Lee brought her back and annulled the marriage, but that didn't change *her.*" I was rather proud of Ellen's character; she would not be controlled by anyone.

"How did Verbena's nephew turn out?"

Camilla frowned. "He became an alcoholic and later died in an accident. Even so, he was the catch of the season, and everyone thought he had a great future ahead of him. He was rich and in the Foreign Service, his father had been Ambassador to Italy, and what with Verbena's influence and so on he could have risen to great heights."

"But he *did* take to drink."

"Even so, no one knew it at the time. Ellen had no business walking out."

"Perhaps she suspected what his future might be; it looks as though she had better sense than her father."

Camilla shook her head stubbornly; then, with woman's logic: "Besides, he might not have been an alcoholic if she had married him. Well, her parents never forgave her for that particulcar scandal, and then after she began to have men friends of all sorts they sent her away to New York, where that sort of thing isn't so noticeable." Talisman City suddenly showed its bleak intolerant head, besprinkled with hay-seed and moral rectitude. I saw no reason to defend Ellen, who is a bit of a madwoman about sex; on the ohter hand, Camilla's high and mighty line did not accord with her own behaviour. It was obvious she hated Ellen and would use any stick to beat her with, and Ellen always proffered a formidable mace for this purpose to anyone hostilely minded.

"Tell me," I said, a little maliciously, "why do you think Rufus killed your father?"

She was startled. "Why Rufus . . . but obviously because of that business deal, the one Johnson's involved in, too.

At least that's what Winters said. Rufus was to cover up for the others; he was to take the blame."

"But now it's all in the newspapers and Rufus is *not* taking the blame."

"Then why did he say he was going to in his confession?"

"Perhaps because someone else wrote it for him, after killing him."

Her eyes grew round. "You're not suggesting that Rufus was killed, too?"

"It's possible."

"But who would want to kill him?"

"The same man who murdered your father."

"But that man was Rufus."

"There was a time when you weren't so sure."

Even in the gloom, I could see her flush. "That's not fair," she said in a small voice.

"Why did you think your husband killed the Senator?" I closed in, aware of my advantage.

"I told you. I was upset, hysterical . . ."

"Why did you think he did it?"

"For . . . for the same reason everyone else did, because of the contracts running out, because Lee wouldn't help him."

"Yet you knew that the contract had already been secured through someone else."

"Verbena told you that, didn't she?" Out it shot, before she could stop herself. She bit her lip.

I was slowly getting the picture, all the background was in a last: now for the foreground, to fill in the shadowy outline at the puzzle's centre, to construct the murderer. I was growing nervous with excitement.

I controlled my voice, though, sounded off-hand. "Yes, as a matter of fact, Verbena did mention to me that she

162

had helped Pomeroy get his government contract before he came to Washington to see Lee. . . ."

"That wasn't wise of her at all. These things are so delicate; it could affect our whole business. That was why Roger said nothing about it even after they arrested him."

"If you knew that he had no real quarrel with the Senator, that he wasn't ruined, why did you tell me that night that he was the murderer?"

"Because," she had regained control of herself now, "because I didn't know until the next day that his contract *was* set. He told me when it looked as if he might be arrested any minute. He knew that I adored my father more than anyone else in the world. He knew that I had lost my head when he was murdered, and I think he knew, also, though he never mentioned it, that I suspected him of the murder, to get even with Lee, to get my inheritance . . . so he broke an old rule of his and told me about his business, about how he had gone to Verbena and she had helped him, despite the Senator. Then I knew how absurd the whole case against him really was. . . ."

"But you had come to me and told me you thought he was the murderer."

"I thought he was, yes. I thought he'd gone mad. I thought he'd kill *me* next to get the inheritance. I thought he was desperate, and so I went off my head for twenty-four hours. It was just too much, having everybody know I was Lee's daughter; everything was so awful that I . . . I came to your room. I don't know why, but I did. For some reason I was afraid Roger might kill me that night. I . . . was terribly ashamed afterwards."

There seemed nothing more to clear up here. Her story was accurate, as far as I could tell. It was also revelatory. Verbena Pruitt began to loom large in the background. What was her rôle in all this? I had never suspected that she would ever seem mysterious to me. I had under-estimated her.

I was ready now to end the session with Camilla Pomeroy; unfortunately we had to go through a number of gyrations which propriety, at least in Talisman City, demands of those who have known one another's bodies.

I told her that knowing her had been one of the most wonderful events of my life and that I hoped we should meet again soon.

She told me that I had helped her more than she could say, at a desperate moment. She asked me to forgive her for what she had done. Not entirely sure for which of her treacheries she desired forgiveness, I delivered myself of a blanket absolution. Then, our love affair put on ice, as it were, each with a beautiful memory, she pressed my hand and left me to pay the cheque.

When I got to the lobby she was gone. I was about to call a cab when I saw two familiar figures in serious talk, half hidden by a potted tree. I went over and said hello to Elmer Bush and Johnson Ledbetter, the Senator-Designate and perhaps never-to-be.

They both looked as though I was the last person in the world they wanted to see at this moment. The falling statesman looked puffy-eyed and tired. The journalist looked eager, like an opportunistic tiger courting a lost sheep. They were cooking up some scheme.

"How are you today, 'Senator'?" I said brightly; even the falling statesman got the quotes.

"Very well, Sargeant." I was surprised he remembered my name.

"This is a grave crisis," said Elmer Bush in his best doom voice.

"A misunderstanding," said Ledbetter in a strangled voice.

"We hope, however, to have the truth before the public tonight, on my programme," said Elmer tightly.

"I hope, sir, that you will be vindicated."

"Thank you, my boy," said Ledbetter in a husky voice. At that moment the famous newspaper-man's cry: "There he is!" was heard in the lobby, somewhat muffled out of deference to the Mayflower's dignity; and a journalist and photographer came pounding towards us, their rimless spectacles gleaming, their faces red from cold and pleasure as they cornered the falling star.

"It has all been," intoned Johnson Ledbetter, "a fantastic mistake."

2

Fantastic mistake or not, it was the main conversation in Washington these days and, to read the newspapers, everywhere else, too. Corruption when it stains senatorial togas, always ceases to becomes squalid and becomes tragical, as Mr. Ledbetter would say.

After leaving the Mayflower, I went to the house of Mrs. Goldmountain, knowing that she was to be at home this afternoon. She was, I had discovered, a good source of information, having spent the better part of her fifty years climbing upwards socially; along the way she had investigated nearly every eminent cupboard in Washington society she was also proving to be a source of revenue to me as far as the Heigh-Ho Dog Food Company went.

I was led to the yellow room where I found her in deep conversation with that Vice-President of Heigh-Ho to whom I had spoken the day before.

As I entered, she was saying: "Hermione has a range of four octaves, of which three are usable."

"But that's marvellous," said the official, a doggish-looking man, constructed on the order of a chow.

"Mr. Sargeant, I'm so happy you came by, and just at this moment, too. I'm sure your ears must've been burning."

"Pete, here, knows what we think of him at Heigh-Ho," said the chow, beaming, handing me his damp squashy paw to shake; I shook it quickly and let it drop. I bowed a moment over Mrs. G's hand, the way diplomats are supposed to do.

"In many ways," said the chow, 'this will be the most novel public relations stunt of the age. You realise that?"

"That's what I'm paid for," I said modestly, making a mental note to arrange to take a percentage of the gross on Hermione's various activities; I was wondering whether an agent's fee, as well, would be too exorbitant, when Mrs. Goldmountain recalled me from my greed.

"Although I am, in principle, opposed to Self-Exploitation, I couldn't, in all conscience, allow my girl not to take advantage of this wonderful opportunity, nor could I be so cruel as to keep her talent under a bushel."

I refrained from commenting that that was probably just where it belonged, under the biggest heaviest bushel there was.

"You've taken the right line," said the official gravely, impressed by Mrs. Goldmountain's wealth and hard-earned social position, *and* excellent press relations; all that glitters is not a gold-mountain, I felt like telling him, but then it was to my interest to keep the farce going.

"Have you made arrangements about engaging Town Hall?"

He nodded. "It's all being prepared now. I'm lining up the press. We'll have a full coverage."

"I can do all that," I said quickly. "That's my job, after all."

"There'll be a lot for you to do; don't worry. Heigh-Ho, however, is getting behind this campaign with everything it's got. We may even take radio time." The noise of money coming my way, lulled me for a moment, like the sirens singing; but then, before I knew it, Hermione and not the sirens was singing.

She had been brought into the large drawing-room next to the yellow room and her accompanist had begun to play. A long yowl chilled my blood, more chilling was the fact that, despite the unmistakable canine quality of the voice, Hermione had perfect pitch. She was not, however, a trained musician.

Mrs. Goldmountain looked dreamily towards the open door through which floated, or rather raced, the poodle's voice. "She practises every day . . . not too long, though. I don't want her to strain her voice."

"Maybe we ought to insure it," said the dog-faced purveyor anxiously, "wouldn't want anything to happen to her. Lloyd's would be only too glad to oblige us."

"If you like . . . though I'm sure nothing will happen; she is always under the closest supervision."

Hermione screamed her way through the 'Bell Song' from *Lakmé* and, my nerves in tatters, my ears vibrating like beaten drums, I applauded loudly, along with the official from Heigh-Ho. Mrs. Goldmountain only smiled.

Then, after several points of business had been cleared up, Mrs. Goldmountain and I were left alone: the official gone back to New York to make an announcement to the news services, Hermilone gone back to her quarters and the tin of *fois gras* to which she was often treated after singing.

It took me some time to get the subject off Hermione and

167

back to the Rhodes family or rather to Ledbetter who now occupied my hostess's thoughts.

"Johnson called me on the phone this morning (we're very close, you know); he sounded simply awful."

"I know, I saw him at the Mayflower this afternoon. He was with Elmer Bush."

"At least Elmer will stand by him through thick and thin. Johnson will need friends." I allowed that this was probably the case.

"This morning I telephoned the Vice-President to tell him that I was confident Johnson had done nothing wrong."

"What did the Vice-President say?"

"Oh, he was on the floor. I didn't get him but his secretary said she would give him my message."

"Well, according to all accounts he seems guilty of fraud, along with the other two."

"I doubt it, but then I must confess I never read the newspapers . . . at least the political sections; those people are always writing lies about personal friends of mine, and then they never know what's going on until it's already happened." She smiled sphinx-like, implying she *did* know; and perhaps she did.

"In any case, he probably won't be allowed to take his seat."

"I'm sure they'll be able to arrange it," she said confidently. "They need him, you know."

I didn't pursue this point.

"I blame that dreadful little man, the secretary, the one who killed himself, for everything. I'm sure he did it deliberately . . . made up all sorts of documents just to implicate Johnson. He was a nasty creature, I always thought, killing Lee like that and then purposely framing poor Johnson." This was a novel twist.

"Did you know him at all?"

"Who? The secretary? Hardly, but I never liked his looks those few times I saw him. Johnson is building his case on the little man's dishonesty, however. He swears to me that it's a deliberate plot and I believe him. He quarrelled with him the night he died."

"Who quarrelled with whom?"

"Johnson and that little man, you know, Hollister."

"How do you know?"

"Johnson told me. He tells me everything, not that's it's any particular secret; soon everyone will know it."

"But where did this take place?" Veils were trembling before my eyes; the figure at the puzzle's centre grew more distinct.

"Johnson spent the evening at the Rhodes's, with Mrs. Rhodes, the evening Hollister killed himself. Didn't you see him? But of course not, you were at my party and Johnson should have been there, too, except he rightly decided that his first evening in Washington as a Senator should be spent with his predecessor's widow, a very, very nice thing to do, but then Johnson is a nice man."

"You mean he was in the house when Hollister died?"

"But of course and he had, he tells me, a private conversation with Hollister of the most unpleasant kind."

"Without witnesses?"

"There would hardly be witnesses if the conversation was private."

"I wonder why the papers didn't mention that he was in the house when the murder took place."

"Perhaps no one thought to tell them . . . they never know anything."

For a while I entertained the mad fantasy that Verbena Pruitt, Mrs. Rhodes and the Senator-Designate (the only three in the house at the time, other than servants) might have got together and killed Rufus on their own. Each had a motive, except perhaps Verbena. The vision, however, of these three elderly political figures tiptoeing upstairs to shoot Rufus Hollister was much too ludicrous.

I arrived at the house shortly before dinner. It was already dark outside and the curtains were drawn against the night. The plain-clothes man who usually stood guard was nowhere in sight.

In the drawing-room I found Mrs. Rhodes, quite alone, playing solitaire at a tiny Queen Anne desk. She greeted me with her usual neutrality.

"I suppose," I said, "you'll be glad to see the last of us."

"The last of you under these circumstances," she replied courteously, motioning me to sit beside her.

"What do you plan to do when all this is over, when the estate is settled and everything is taken care of?"

"Do?" she looked at me blankly for a moment, as though she had not, until now, conceived there would be a future.

"I mean do you intend to go back to Talisman City, or live here?"

She gave me a long look, as though I had asked her a nearly impossible question. Finally she said: "I shall stay here of course. All my friends are here," she added mechanically.

"Like Mrs. Goldmountain?"

She smiled suddenly, for the first time since I met her, like sun on the snow. "No, not like Mrs. Goldmountain. Others . . . my old friends from the early days. We had no very close friends back home, the old ones died off and we made no new ones, except politically. I haven't lived there since we came to Washington."

"I saw Mrs. Goldmountain today."

"Yes?" She was clearly not interested.

"I understand she's a great friend of Governor Ledbetter's."

"I believe so."

"She is certainly taking his side in this business."

"As she should. I'm sure that Johnson did nothing dishonest, nor did Lee." But this came out automatically; she seemed to be making a series of prepared responses, her mind on something else.

"I didn't know the Governor was here the night Rufus died."

"Oh yes, we had a nice chat. He is a good friend, you know, as well as our lawyer."

"He told Mrs. Goldmountain that he and Rufus quarrelled that night, about the business of those companies."

Mrs. Rhodes frowned. "Ida Goldmountain should show better sense," she said sharply. "Yes, they had a disagreement. Over what I don't know; it took place upstairs, in Rufus's room."

"Did the police know this?"

"That Johnson was here? Oh yes, both Verbena and I told them when we were questioned as to who was in the house."

"Did they know that the Governor went upstairs to talk to Rufus, alone? That they quarrelled?"

She looked at me coldly, with sudden dislike. "Why, I don't know," she said. "The police didn't ask me and I don't remember having volunteered any information. I am so used to having things misunderstood," she said and her voice was hard.

171

"I'm sure they must know," I said thoughtfully, trying to figure out Winters: why had he kept this piece of information secret? Not only from me but from the official report given to the newspapers.

"Besides," she said, "the case ended when Rufus killed himself. There was no need to involve one's friends any more than was necessary. I appreciated Johnson's kindness in coming to see me his first night in Washington, before he was to take his seat. If I were you," and she looked at me with her clear onyx eyes, unmarked by age or disaster, "I would say nothing about Johnson's exchange with Rufus."

"I'll have no occasion to, yet," I said, quite cool as the old lady. "In any case, I'm not the person to silence. Mrs. Goldmountain is. She's the informer."

"That fool!" Mrs. Rhodes exploded.

"Fool or not, she's given us a new angle on the case."

"Case?" what case?"

"On who killed your husband, Mrs. Rhodes, and who killed Rufus Hollister."

She sat back in her chair: "You're mad," she said in a low voice. "It's all over. The police are satisfied. *Leave it alone,*" her voice was harshly urgent.

"But the police aren't satisfied," I said, and this was a big and dangerous guess. "They know as well as you and I that Rufus was killed; they are waiting for the real murderer to make some move. So am I."

"I don't believe you."

"But it's true."

"Even if all you say is true why do you involve yourself in it? Why not go back to New York? Why involve yourself in a world which has nothing to do with yours?"

"Because, Mrs. Rhodes, I'm already involved, because I'm in danger no matter where I go."

"Danger? Why?"

"Because I know who the murderer is and the murderer knows that I know." This was a crashing lie but there was no help for it.

She pushed her chair back and stood up, as though prepared to run from the room; her face was ash-grey. "You're lying." she said at last.

I stood up, too. From the hall I could hear a door shut and the sound of someone running upstairs. We stood looking at one another like two graven images, like gargoyles on a medieval tower.

Then she recovered her composure and gave a strange little laugh. "You are trying to confuse me," she said, attempting lightness. "We all know that Rufus was the murderer and that he killed himself. Whatever the argument Johnson had with him was perfectly innocent . . . as far as the main thing goes. Certainly the thought that Johnson killed Rufus is a ridiculous one, quite unimaginable."

"Then why did *you* imagine it, Mrs. Rhodes? It never occurred to me that he did."

She flushed, confused. "I . . . I was mistaken then. I was under the impression you thought Johnson was in some way involved."

I was conscious that she had betrayed something of enormous value to me, but what I could not tell. "No," I said. "I never thought the Governor killed Rufus, but I am curious about their conversation."

"I suspect that it is none of your business, in any case, Mr. Sargeant," Mrs. Rhodes was herself again.

"As I pointed out, it *is* my business if it concerns the murder." I could be quite as cold as she.

"And you think there is some connection?"

"Certainly. The collapse of this company has a great deal

to do with the case . . . not only with your husband's death but with the career of Governor Ledbetter."

She gathered up her purse, a handkerchief, prepared to go. "I assume then you will be staying with us for quite some time, after the others leave tomorrow?" This was insulting.

"No, Mrs. Rhodes," I said looking her straight in the eye, "I will deliver the murderer tomorrow."

She looked at me for one long moment, quite expressionless; then in a low voice, intensely, she said: "You meddlesome fool!" and she swept out of the room.

Feeling somewhat shaken, and a little silly, I went out into the hall. A familiar perfume was in the air as I walked slowly up the stairs, wondering what to do next. There was very little chance that I would be able to unmask the the murderer, much less be able to collect sufficient evidence to assure conviction.

I was tempted to forget about the whole thing.

I was surprised, when I opened the door to my room, to find Walter Langdon leaning over my desk in a most incriminating fashion. He gave a jump when he saw me.

"Oh! I . . . I'm awfully sorry. I came in here just a minute ago, looking for you. I wanted to borrow some typewriter paper."

At least it could have been a match, or wanting to know the time. "There's some in the top drawer," I said.

He opened it and, with shaking hands, took out a few sheets. "Thanks a lot."

"Perfectly all right."

"Hope I can do the same for you one day."

"Never can tell." The sort of dialogue which insures, or used to insure, any number of Hollywood script-writers a secure and large income.

"Sit down," I said.

"I really better get ready for dinner."

"You look just fine." He sat down in the chair at the desk; I sat on the foot of the bed, legs crossed in a most nonchalant fashion. "Are you satisfied with the way things turned out?"

He looked puzzled. "You mean the murders?"

I caught that. "So you think Rufus was murdered too?"

"No, he killed himself, didn't he? That's what the police seem to think."

"Why did you say 'murders'?"

"A slip of the tongue. Two deaths is what I meant." He was perfectly calm.

"But I take it you think Rufus was murdered?"

"You take it wrong, Sargeant," said Langdon. "I see no reason to think Rufus might have been killed. It makes perfect sense the way it is. I think you should leave it alone." The second time I had been advised, in exactly those words, to keep my nose clean. I was beginning to feel that a monstrous cabal had been formed to misguide me.

"You don't have much of the newspaper-man in you, Langdon," I said in the hearty tone of a stock company actor in *The Front Page*.

"I'm not really one," said Langdon with a touch of frost in his voice. "I just do occasional articles. I'm mainly interested in the novel."

I have all the pseudo-intellectual's loathing of those who have dedicated themselves, no matter how sincerely and competently, to art . . . a form of envy, I suppose, which becomes contempt if they fail. Langdon had all the ear-marks of a potential disaster.

"Even so you should be more interested in this sort of thing. Have you decided what you're going to write about for your magazine?"

He nodded. "I'm working on it now, that's why I needed the paper. I want to have a first draft ready by the time I get back to the office, tomorrow afternoon."

"What line are you taking?"

*"Oh, the implications of a political murder . . . I use the Rhodes thing as a point of departure, if you know what I mean."

I knew only too well: the Diachotomy of Murder or The Theology of Crisis in Reaction. It would be great fun to read, I decided grimly. "Then you'll be taking the noon train with Ellen?" This was a guess, but perfectly logical.

"Yes, as a matter of fact, we *are* going back together."

"She's quite something isn't she?"

Langdon nodded seriously. "She certainly is."

"Are you still engaged to her?"

"Oh, it wasn't a formal engagement."

"I'm sure of that; they never are."

Langdon blushed. "She . . . she's very promiscuous, isn't she?"

"Yes, Walter, she is," I said in the tone of a Scout-master explaining to a new tenderfoot the parts of the body and their uses.

"I didn't think it was so bad until we went out to Chevy Chase and she ducked off with a marine . . ."

"She's been known to complete a seduction in ten minutes."

"Well, this took a lot longer. I was mad as hell at her but she told me it was none of my business, that she thought the marine much too nice-looking to let go; it was then I caught on."

"You didn't really care about her that much, did you?" I was curious; both Ellen and I had thought him a fool.

He scratched his sandy hair in a bumpkin manner. "Not

really. I never ran into anything quite like her before and I guess I was taken in for a little bit."

"The fact she now has a million dollars, as well as an uninhibilted technique, might make her irresistible to an American boy."

"Not this boy." But I detected a wistful note; she had used him up, as it were. I wondered what would become of her now that she was rich; there were bound to be operators cleverer than she in the world, and what a ride they could take her for. Well, it was no business of mine.

"Let me see what you write for the *Advanceguard,* if you don't mind."

"Not at all. I'd like your advice." Then he left the room.

I pottered about the room, getting ready for dinner, the last dinner in this house. I packed my bag, slowly, reluctantly, aware that the puzzle was incomplete and would doubtless remain so now, for ever. I cursed my ill luck, my slow brain, the craft of my opponent: for some time now I had regarded the killer as a malicious personal opponent whose delight it was to torment me.

I opened my desk to see if there were any letters or old socks in the drawers. There was nothing. Only a few sheets of typewriter paper. On one of them I had made some elaborate doodles; at the centre of the largest decoration I had written "paper-chase" in old English type.

Paper-chase. I thought of Mrs. Rhodes. Something I had heard that day came back to me, something I had known all along appeared in a new way. Unexpectedly every piece fell into place.

And I knew who had killed Senator Rhodes, and Rufus Hollister.

4

It was evident from the happy faces at table that night that this was to be our last supper together. No one was sorry that the ghastly time was finally over. I was giddy with triumph and I had a difficult time not showing it. My exuberance was doubtless attributed to our coming freedom. We were like prisoners on the eve of parole.

I took great care not to betray myself. I made no reference all that evening to the case; I indicated in no way that I had completed the jigsaw puzzle. I even refrained from staring too long at the killer, who was most serene, doubtless confident that the whole desperate gamble had been won at last.

Winters was noticeable by his absence. There had been some talk that he would come by to say farewell but he did not, out of shame at facing me, I decided, complacent in my victory, keyed up to an extraordinary pitch both by my discovery and by the danger which attended it.

I lacked evidence, of course, but when one knows a problem's answer its component parts can be deduced *and* proved, by working backwards. I had, I was sure, the means of proving what I knew.

After dinner, we were joined in the drawing-room by Johnson Ledbetter and Elmer Bush. They came in out of the black winter night, their faces red from cold, bringing cold air with them.

Their entrance depressed, somewhat, the gala mood of the guests.

Mrs. Rhodes poured us coffee. Cups were handed about. The discredited statesman took bourbon. His journalistic ally did the same. They sat talking by the fire to Mrs. Rhodes, Roger Pomeroy and Verbena Pruitt, leaving the women and children to amuse themselves. We amused ourselves, even though I was anxious to join the circle by the fire.

Ellen and Camilla fell to wrangling in a most sisterly fashion while Langdon and I exchanged weighty opinions on the state of contemporary letters ('decadent').

After an hour of this, everyone shifted positions, as often happens with a group in civilised society: a spontaneous re-arrangement of the elements to distribute the boredom more democratically.

I ended up with Ledbetter and Elmer and Verbena Pruitt at the fireplace.

"It has become," said Ledbetter slowly, "A Party Issue."

"In which case you're bound to win," said Verbena comfortably. "I have word that the White House intends to intervene."

"But when? When?" His voice rose querulously.

"*His* hands are tied. You know how *he* feels about interfering in legislative problems. Yet I have it on the highest, the very highest, authority that *he* intends to act before the week is over. One word from *him* and the Party will support you."

"Meanwhile I undergo martyrdom."

"It may turn out to be political Capital," said Elmer Bush, nodding happily, pleased to be involved in such high and dirty politics.

The Senator-Designate snorted. He looked at the end of his rope; he was also getting tight. "What a mess it is, Grace," he said, turning with a sigh to Mrs. Rhodes. She smiled and patted his hand.

"It won't last much longer," she said softly.

"I hope you're right." I was surprised by this sudden gentle exchange; could they have been . . . but it was too far-fetched.

I was suddenly tempted to drop the whole thing; to retire

from the scene with the secret satisfaction of having solved a case which, all things considered, had proven to be damned near insoluble.

I looked at the murderer thoughtfully, aware, disagreeably, of my own power. I have few sadistic impulses and I had no chivalrous love for any of the dead. I resolved at that moment to keep my information to myself.

"The point I have been making continually," said Ledbetter, turning on the professional political voice which became him so well, if you happen to like politicians of the old school, "is that my connection with the company was perfectly legal, that Rufus and Lee between them ran it and that all I did was have my office occasionally handle their legal work for them. I had no other connection with it."

"But why, Senator, if you had so little to do with the companies, did you have an equal share with Mr. Rhodes?" I was surprised at my own boldness; hostile eyes were turned upon me.

"I left all that to them, young man. Instead of paying me a legal fee, they gave me stock. I paid very little attention to what they were doing. I will not say that I was used by Lee, my oldest and dearest friend, but I *will* say that Rufus Hollister was a most sinister figure. I am now engaged in investigating, at considerable expense, his business dealing for the past fifteen years, since he came to Washington. It will make unsavoury reading, sir, most unsavoury."

Elmer Bush nodded. "There is already enough proof at hand to show that Hollister was involved, on his own, in a number of rackets which would completely discredit him."

"While my own record is . . . " "An open book" I murmured to myself, "an open book," said Johnson Letbetter, scowling honestly. "I was used by him. I am being used now by politicians in an effort to discredit not only me but the Party. We will win, though," he added, his voice solemn, like a keynoter at a convention.

"You should've shown more sense," said Verbena sharply. Mrs. Rhodes excused herself, aware, doubtless, that her husband's memory might be impugned. It was. "Lee was always getting involved in some get-rich-quick scheme and though he was perfectly honest he couldn't resist a deal, no matter how shady, if it looked like a million dollars might be made. The fact that he never made a cent on these things is proof enough that he was a dupe himself, though he thought he was a financial genius."

"Where did he make that three and a half million he left in his will?" I asked, always practical.

"Inherited," said Verbena crisply.

This was interesting; I wondered why I had never thought before to inquire into the source of the Rhodes fortune. "One thing which puzzles me, though," I said, in a very humble way, "is why, if Senator Rhodes was perfectly innocent in this deal, did he go out of his way to arrange it so that Rufus Hollister would be solely responsible for the company's illegality?"

"How," said Ledbetter, "do we know that Lee did? We have only Hollister's word for it, in that farewell note of his."

"We have also those documents which were sent to me anonymously.

"Had they been executed?"

"No, sir, they had not, but the fact that they had been drawn up indicated that someone expected to use them in case the various deals were ever made public; the papers provided a perfect out for Rhodes." And for you, I added to myself.

"But there is no proof that either Lee or myself drew up

181

those documents, remember that," said Ledbetter, and I saw quite clearly the direction his defence would take.

"By the way," I asked, "what was his attitude the other night when you talked to him, before he died?"

The Senator-Designate was startled.

Verbena snorted angrily. "How did you know Johnson was here?"

"It's no secret, is it?"

"At the moment, yes," said Verbena and she looked like an angry mountain before an eruption.

"You will do me a great favour by saying nothing about that visit in the press, my boy," said Ledbetter with an attempt at good-fellowship.

"I'm sure Pete wouldn't think of it," said Elmer, warningly: reminding me that he was still author of the *Globe's* main feature: 'America's New York', and of considerable influence with the editor.

"I have no intention of printing any of this, Senator," I said earnestly. "My only interest was in the murder. Politics is out of my line. I was only curious, that's all. I mean you *were* the last person to see Rufus alive."

"This is, then, off the record," said Ledbetter heavily "Rufus Hollister threatened me, threatened to blackmail me. I told him to do his worst. He said he would, that he would cause a scandal, even if it would involve him. I am afraid that we parted enemies, never to meet again in this world." There was a long silence.

I was suddenly weary of the whole business, sleepy, too. Mrs. Rhodes returned and the company rearranged itself like musical chairs. I refused a drink, was given coffee, but it did not wake me up. Yawning widely behind my hand, I excused myself and went up to bed.

The case was solved and I had the satisfaction not only of having solved it but also of denying myself the glory of announcing my solution to the world, to the accompaniment of fame and glory. I was quite pleased with myself. When I got to my room, I went straight to the bathroom to brush my teeth. I was so exhausted that I had trouble keeping awake. When I finished I sat down for a moment on the toilet seat to rest. I awoke suddenly to find that my head had fallen with a crack against the wash-basin. I had gone to sleep.

Rubbing my eyes, I got to my feet and went into the bedroom. Each step I took fatigued me. I wondered if I might be ill, if I'd caught Camilla Pomeroy's virus. I fell across the bed. I was ill. I tried to sit up but the effort was too great. My hands and feet were ice-cold and I felt chill waves engulf my body.

Clouded as my brain was, on the verge of unconsciousness, I realised that I had been poisoned. I was just able to knock the telephone off its hook before I passed out.

SEVEN

I

"Is he dead?" asked Lieutenant Winters, his voice coming to me from behind some dark green clouds through which a light shone fitfully..

"Not yet," said a voice and I slipped away, discouraged.

My next attempt at consciousness occurred when a great many yards of tubing were withdrawn from my insides. I opened my eyes, saw a pair of hands above me, felt the tube being withdrawn, felt hideously sick and passed out again.

The next day, however, I was sitting up in bed ready to receive callers. My head ached terribly and I was extremely weak. Otherwise my mind, such as it is, was functioning smoothly.

A trained nurse was the first person I saw on my return to the vale of tears. She smiled cheerfully. "They took out two quarts," she said.

I moaned.

"Now it's not as bad as all that."

I said that it was as bad as all that. I asked her what time it was. "Eleven forty-seven. You can have milk toast now if you want it."

I said that it was unlikely I should ever want milk toast at any time; in fact, the whole idea of food, despite the complete vacuum in my stomach, was sickening. I asked if it was day or night.

"Daytime, silly."

"How long have I been unconscious?"

"About ten hours, since last night. You came to once or twice while Doctor was pumping your stomach; you made things very difficult for Doctor."

"For Nurse, too, I'll bet," I said, remembering my hospital-talk from an appendectomy of some years before.

"I'm used to difficult cases," she said with some pride. "We had a very difficult case, Doctor and, I, a week ago. It involved a total castration and by gracious . . ."

"Send for Lieutenant Winters," I said weakly, putting a halt to these dreadful reminiscences.

"Well, I'm not sure that . . ."

"I will get up and go to him myself," I said, sitting up with a great effort.

She grew alarmed. "You stay right there, dear, and I'll go get him. Now don't you move." I couldn't have moved if I wanted to.

A moment later she returned with Winters. He looked upset; as well he should have been. He motioned for the angel of mercy to leave the room.

When we were alone, he said: "Why did you do it?"

"Why did I do what?"

"Take all those sleeping tablets. According to the doctor, you took over a dozen of the strongest type. If you hadn't knocked the receiver off the hook and the butler heard the phone ring in the pantry, you would've been dead now, which, I suppose, is what you intended to do."

"Winters," I said softly, "when I go you go with me."

He looked alarmed. "What do you mean?"

"Only that I did not take any sleeping-tablets, that I was deliberately poisoned."

"Are you sure of this?"

I called him several insulting names. He took them gravely, as though trying to determine whether or not they suited him.

185

"Who do you think gave them to you, and how?"

"They were given me by the killer you failed to apprehend and, as for how, they were slipped rather cleverly into the coffee I drank after dinner. Mrs. Rhodes serves something which tastes not unlike Turkish mud, very expensive and heavy, so heavy that it's impossible to taste whether it's been tampered with or not."

"Why do you think you were poisoned?"

"Because I know who did the murders."

"You do not." Winters sounded suddenly like an angry schoolboy trying to put a braggart in his place.

"I do, too," I said, mocking his tone. He blushed.

"I didn't mean it like that. I just don't see how you happen to know who did the murder from the information available."

"It may be that I have a better mind than yours."

It was his turn to attribute rude characteristics to me. I smiled seraphically all through his insults. When he finished, I suggested that this was hardly the way to speak to a man who has only recently returned from the other side. Then, all passion spent, I spoke to him reasonably. "As soon as I have enough evidence I'll let you know."

"When will that be?"

"Tonight at dinner," I said gaily, not at all sure that I could produce enough evidence but undisturbed by any thought of failure: so great is the love of life. I had recovered; I was not to die just yet. It is a feeling common to soldiers and those who survive operations and accidents of a serious nature.

"I insist you tell me now." Winters became suddenly official.

"Not a chance in the world, friend," I said, pulling myself up in bed. My head still ached but I was no longer dizzy. "Now you tell the doctor to give me a shot of something to

186

put a little life back into me and then, like Dr. Holmes, full of morphine or whatever it was he took, I shall proceed to arrange the evidence in such a manner that not even the police will be confused."

"You're out of your mind."

"Will you do as I tell you?"

"No. If someone did try to kill you, and I have only your word that they did, the police would never allow you to be without protection."

"You may protect me as much as you like."

"Damn it, man, you're witholding evidence from the proper authorities, do you realise that? Will you stop playing detective long enough to allow us to do our job properly?"

I was irritated by this. "If you'd done your job properly Rufus Hollister would not be dead and I would be feeling much more fit than I do. Since you can't be trusted to do it on your own, I prefer to do it myself.

Winters bit his lower lip furiously. It took him a second to regain control of his temper. His voice shook when at last he spoke. "I have my own methods, Sargeant. I know what I'm doing. I was perfectly aware that there was a good chance Hollister had been murdered. But we must be thorough. We can't go off after every hare-brained theory which occurs to us, even if it happens to be the right one. We have to build slowly and carefully. It happens that at this moment we are on the verge of some new evidence which may bring us closer to the murderer, assuming Hollister was not a suicide. Amateur help is not much use because amateurs usually end up dead. We were fortunate, I suppose, that we could save *you*." This was a good point and I softened considerably.

"I am," I said, "very moved by your rhetoric. The fact that you people saved my life is one point in your favour.

So we'll make a bargain. I will get up today. I will collect what evidence I need and contrive, if possible, a trap . . . one which will be sprung tonight. I will then, if successful, give Lieutenant Winters full credit for the amazing apprehension of a clever killer. Does that satisfy you?"

It did not satisfy him. We fought for half an hour; finally he agreed, but only after I told him that even if he arrested me I would never reveal what I knew in any way except my own. Reluctantly, he consented. He insisted on following me about all day and I said that he could.

He then called in the nurse who called the doctor who gave me several shots; the nurse then brought me bread and milk which she insisted I eat. Winters excused himself. He would, he said, join me when I was dressed.

"Come on, dear, finish the nice bread." Nurse did everything but stuff the concoction down my throat. I found to my surprise that I liked it, that it restored the lining to my stomach. The return of bulk made me gurgle pleasantly; it was nice to have the body functioning again and my head felt less sore.

"Now, you rest there like a good boy for twenty minutes before you get up. Doctor's orders. Shots must have time to take effect." With that she was gone. As she went out the door, I saw that a plain-clothes man was standing guard over me. I closed my eyes and breathed deeply, preparing myself for the battle ahead. It was going to be a full day.

There was a sudden commotion outside the door and I heard Ellen's clear commanding voice ring out over the gruff tones of the law: "I insist on seeing him. He happens to be my fiancé."

"Let her in!" I shouted; the door was opened and Ellen swept in.

"Bloody oaf," she said, plumping down in the chair

188

beside the bed. Her voice softened. "Poor darling! You tried to kill yourself for love of me, didn't you?"

"I couldn't bear the thought of you and Walter Langdon living together in Garden City with a dog and little ones."

"I should've known that I wasn't the cause of your suicide. I never am. No man ever seems to want to kill himself on my account."

"Someone tried to kill *me,* though, on general principle, I suspect."

Ellen frowned suddenly and looked nervously at the door, as though expecting a gunman to be lurking there. Then: "Rufus was killed, wasn't he?"

"I nodded.

"And the same person who killed him killed my father and tried to poison you?" I nodded again. She looked thoughtful. "I figured that out some time ago. I didn't believe the story that you tried to kill yourself."

"Was that what the police said?" I was incredulous.

"Of course . . . they'd hardly admit their case wasn't closed."

I whistled. "Winters is pretty smart. If I had died he would have said I was a suicide and that would've been the end of the case . . . everything would be just ducky."

"They're so corrupt," said Ellen, betraying more feeling for me than I had thought possible.

"I wonder why Winters didn't let me quietly drift off to a better world?"

"Because, my darling, I for one raised such a fuss and summoned the doctor. It was completely a matter of self-esteem. I couldn't take the chance of your killing yourself for me (as Verbena Pruitt maintained you had, out of jealousy over Walter) and then having you actually die and there be some doubt. I insisted you be saved so that the world could hear from your own foam-flecked lips that it

189

was because of me you wanted to end it all. How in demand I should've been!" She chuckled: then, seriously, slowly, "Peter, do be careful. Of all my fiancés I am fondest of you, at this moment anyway. For God's sake be careful."

"I will, dear. I have no intention of letting myself get killed."

"You haven't done so well so far," she said. She paused; when finally she spoke, her voice trembled and for the first time since I'd known her she was no longer in control. "I'm terrified," she whispered. "There's something I should've told you when Father was killed. You remember I said then I knew who did it? Well, in a way, I did. When Mother . . .'

But she wasn't allowed to continue. At that moment the door opened and Mrs. Rhodes entered. "Ah, Ellen, I didn't know you were here." She seemed disagreeably surprised But quickly she became all sympathy, brushing past her daughter to me. "Mr. Sargeant, I do hope you're better; I tried to see you earlier but you were still unconscious."

"It looks as if I'll be all right, Mrs. Rhodes," I said with a gallant smile.

"I'm glad. One more tragedy would have been too horrible to bear."

"It seems," said Ellen, "that he did not kill himself for love of me."

"I never thought he had," said Mrs. Rhodes with a certain sharpness. "Verbena is the romantic one. . . ."

"Well, *if* I had tried to kill myself, Mrs. Rhodes, it would have been for your daughter's sake."

"A pretty speech," said Ellen; she looked drawn and tired.

"Are you getting up now?" asked Mrs. Rhodes.

"Yes, I have an appointment down-town. I'll be back in

time for dinner; you must be so sick of your boarders by now."

"Not at all. In any event, when you come back from your appointment I should like to talk to you." Over her mother's shoulder Ellen shook her head suddenly, warningly.

"I told Mrs. Rhodes that I would be glad to see her later in the afternoon, if we had time. Mother and daughter withdrew.

Carefully I sat up in bed and swung my legs over the edge of the bed. Some fairly discreet fireworks went off in my head. I was weak but not ill. Slowly I dressed. I was tying my tie when Miss Flynn rang me from New York. Her usual composure had obviously suffered a shock.

"You are well?" was her first majestic misuse of an adverb. I told her I had survived, that the report she had read in the newspaper about attempted suicide was not true. I assured her that I would see her the next morning at my office in New York. She was very much relieved. I asked her for news and she told me that all Gotham was Agog at the thought of Hermione's recital. It was generally considered that I had pulled off the public relations stunt of the minute. I told her to contact the editor of the *Globe* and tell him that I should have another article for him on the Rhodes murder case and that, since it would be the eyewitness account of the murderer's arrest, I would expect X number of dollars for this unique bit of coverage. Miss Flynn agreed to Talk Turkey with the *Globe*. "I trust, however, you will be very careful in the course of this most Crucial Day." I said that I would. I then asked her to check, if possible, some records and to call me back at five o'clock. She said that neither rain nor sleet . . . or so many other words, equally prolix . . . would keep her from finding out what I wanted to know.

2

The day went smoothly.

Winters went everywhere I did, but perversely, I kept throwing him off the track, to his fury. He could say nothing, though, for it was part of his official pose that he knew already, on his own, who the murderer was. I am fairly certain that he did not figure it out until the business was finished.

Before I left I requested that Johnson Ledbetter be asked to dinner that night, *without* Elmer Bush.

On our way down-town, I read the afternoon paper. My attempted suicide appeared on page ten, with very little tie-up to the Rhodes affair. The Ledbetter affair occupied the front page, however. He was quoted at length to the effect he had been smeared by the opposition. There was even an editorial on the subject of morality in politics. Everyone was having a good time with all this and none of the papers seemed aware that either the Governor's fiasco or my own misadventure was in any way connected with the recently 'solved' murder. All this was to the good, I thought, with some satisfaction. It would make the beat all the more exciting.

"What's our first stop?" asked Winters.

"Our first stop is the Party Headquarters and the office of one Verbena Pruitt."

"But . . ."

"There will be neither 'buts' nor outcries. You will in fact have to wait outside in the ante-room while I speak to her." There was considerable outcry at this, but I won my point.

Verbena's office was large and comfortable. Its position on the second-floor corner, southern exposure, indicated her importance in the Party. I was allowed to come in right away. Winters waited outside in the hall, trying, no doubt, to listen through the door.

"Come sit over here, beside me," boomed the second or third lady of the land from behind a dainty knee-hole desk which looked as if it might crumple at any moment beneath the weight of her huge arms.

I sat down and she swivelled around in her chair and fixed we with her level agate-gaze. "You look green," she said at last.

"I don't feel so good," I admitted.

"Love!" she snorted. "Root of all evil if you ask me . . . *money* certainly isn't. I'm all for money . . . it's pure; it's useful; you can measure it . . . or at least you could before they started monkeying with the gold standard."

"I didn't kill myself for love, Miss Pruitt."

She brightened. "Money worries? Career on the downgrade?"

"Just the opposite. I was doing too well and someone decided to kill me."

"You're a very daring young man," said Miss Pruitt enigmatically.

"I suppose so. I wish you'd help me, though. There's a lot at stake."

She smiled. "How do you know that *I* may not be 'at stake'?"

"I'm fairly sure. I don't know everything of course; that's why I want you to help me."

To my surprise she said nothing to show that she was surprised by this turn of affairs, that the murderer of Lee Rhodes was still free and dangerous. Instead she said: "Ask me what you like and I'll answer what I like."

"How long did you know Lee Rhodes?"

"Twenty-five years or so."

"Were you in love with him?"

This was daring. She sat back in her swivel chair; I was afraid that it might give way under her, tipping the great lady on her head, but she knew what she was doing. "You're awfully fresh, young man," she said.

"I was curious."

"Then to satisfy your curiosity, yes, we were very close at one time. Shorty after Ellen was born, Lee wanted to divorce Grace and marry me. I may say with some pride that I talked him out of it. We were fond of each other but I was almost as fond of Grace. I didn't want to wreck her life; though, since, I've sometimes wondered if it was the right thing."

"You mean not separating them?"

She nodded, her eyes focused on the far wall, her voice dreamy. "They never got on of course. Grace would've been so much happier with another man, I'm sure of that, but the opportunity never arose again and they settled down with one another, neither contented."

'You went on seeing a great deal of both?"

"Oh yes. I saw them through a hundred crises. When Ellen was supposed to marry that nephew of mine, it was I she came to after her father annulled the marriage. I was the one who reconciled them . . ., though not for long since she went away as soon as she was of age. I practically brought her up. They were the most helpless family you ever saw when it came to managing their private affairs."

"Mrs. Rhodes disliked Camilla, didn't she?"

"Not really. She hated the *idea* of her, naturally, when she found out. Grace is a woman of high principles, you know, and it was a devastating blow for her, finding out Lee had had a by-blow, as they say back home. I think she was quite indifferent to Camilla one way or the other, as a person."

"You obtained the contract for Roger Pomeroy before he came to Washington, didn't you?"

She looked startled. "You're very well informed," she said coldly. "Yes, as a matter of fact I did."

"You must've known all along that he had a pretty good alibi in case of arrest."

"I did. As a matter of fact Grace and Ellen and I discussed the whole thing the morning of the day Pomeroy was to be arrested. I had discovered that that young fool of a policeman was going to arrest Roger and I talked it over with the family: should I or should I not let the police know that I had helped Roger get his contract before he came to see Lee? Roger himself begged me not to. I must say I didn't want to: I would've found myself in a very uncomfortable position. On the other hand, we didn't want Roger arrested. I will tell you, frankly, that none of us knew what to do until Rufus saw fit to kill himself and Roger was released, ending, I may add, one of the worst days of my life."

"Do you think Rufus killed himself?"

"You should know," she said, slowly, looking at me speculatively.

"*I* should know?"

"Did you take sleeping pills?"

"Certainly not."

"Then it would seem Rufus was killed, and the confession was a fake."

"That's how I see it."

"Why would the murderer want to kill you, though?"

"Because I knew everything. I've been poking around, you know, out of curiosity; while nosing about I figured out who did it."

Verbena Pruitt's face was a mask: a vast roseate larger-than-life-size mask. "I can see then why you were poisoned.

Now I will give you some advice: leave Washington. I can promise you that the police will forget the whole thing. There will be no more trouble for any of us. The dead are dead and can't be recalled. The rest of us are well out of it. *You* get out of it, too."

"No."

She was suddenly angry. "What then do you want? What's your price?" This was ugly indeed.

"I'm not for sale," I said, becoming indignant, although my sense of reality didn't entirely desert me even in this heroic moment. "At least not now, to you. I'll tell you one thing, though. I was ready to drop the whole thing last night. I decided it was, as you say, none of my business. I didn't want to upset everyone again. I saw no reason to interfere in an affair which did not, really, concern me at all. But then the murderer tried to kill me and that, for reasons which will become more apparent, was more than I could take. I now intend to turn the killer over to the police."

"When?"

"Tonight."

There was nothing more to say; we were through with one another. I had learned what I needed to know already, earlier in the conversation, and so, very politely, I excused myself and left her office. She did not speak.

"Well?" said Winters, joining me in the corridor.

"Well, yourself, my fine minion of the law."

"Don't be cute."

"It's my nature," I said, feeling blithe.

In the entrance hall we ran into Johnson Ledbetter. He looked more than ever like an harassed buffalo at the end of the trail. He greeted me with hallow vigour. I detached myself from Winters and moved off into a corner with him. Politicos wandering in and out of headquarters quickly averted their gaze when they saw him: he was a fallen star and no one wanted to catch the infection of failure which, as all professionals know, is remarkably contagious.

"We'll be seeing you tonight, won't we, Senator?"

"Yes, of course I'll be there. What's going to happen?"

"We're going to unveil the murderer of Rufus Hollister and Leander Rhodes."

Ledbetter's grey face looked set. "I hope you know what you're doing."

"I do. There's one thing I would like to know, if I may: what *did* happen when you talked to Rufus, before he was shot?"

"That's private."

"You will be forced to tell it to the court, Senator." I was reckless.

"I don't see that it has any bearing on the murders," he said weakly.

"I'm sure Winters can keep you off the witness stand if we know just what happened." I was quite willing to commit Winters to anything at this point.

"We discussed the business of the two companies, all of which you have no doubt read about in the papers."

"What did he have to say?"

"He said we were in danger of being exposed, that a Federal Commission was ready to publish its findings and begin legal proceedings. I said that I, of course, had no connection with any of this, even though my name appeared as a director and there was some stock issued in my name."

"Did Hollister say anything about being exposed?"

"That's all he talked about."

"I mean being exposed by some malicious party, by the murderer?"

Ledbetter paused for one long moment; then he shook his head: "No, he didn't mention anything like that."

"Why did you quarrel?"

"Because he wanted me to accept equal blame with him; since I was not guilty I saw no reason to associate myself with him." This canard was uttered with pious sincerity. "He thought I could get the Party to hush the whole thing up, or at least blame it on Lee. Unfortunately, I couldn't." Ledbetter betrayed himself in a most un-lawyer-like fashion; I wondered how on earth a man of his limited intelligence had managed to become the Governor of a state.

"What time did you go upstairs to talk to him?"

"About eleven-thirty."

"How long were you there?"

"Twenty minutes, I should say."

"Did he act as though he had another appointment?"

Ledbetter's eyes grew wide. "How did you know? Yes, as a matter of fact he did say he was to meet someone at twelve."

"In his room or somewhere else?"

"I assumed some other place since only Verbena, Grace and I were in the house."

"Did you notice anything unusual on you way downstairs?"

He shook his head thoughtfully. "No, I was too angry to pay much attention. It is not a pleasant thing, young man, for a political figure to have his honour impugned and his integrity questioned. I may add that it looks as if I shall soon be vindicated. The Senate committee has already informed me, unofficially, that according to the documentation sent you by the unknown party, I was, along with Lee, the innocent dupe of Rufus Hollister."

198

"Isn't the committee at all interested in discovering who sent me those papers?"

"I don't think the question arose." I trembled for the safety of our country: these were the elders who framed our laws!

"Have you ever wondered who might have sent me those very convenient documents?"

"I'm afraid I've been much too busy to give the matter much thought."

"Well, it was obviously someone who had your interest at heart, as well as a considerable stake in the business of the murders."

"I always assumed that it was sent by a well-wisher who wanted to see justice done."

"A well-wisher who had access to Senator Rhodes's library, who knew where the papers were hidden, who implicated Rufus Hollister, who murdered Rufus Hollister, who mailed the papers to me in a very whimsical fashion, a well-wisher who . . ."

Ledbetter frowned menacingly: "Leave her out of this, hear me? If you drag her into this I'll . . ." But there was no reason to continue our talk and so I excused myself and joined Winters at the door.

"What in the name of God did you tell him? He looked like he was going to kill you."

"Everyone wants to kill me today," I said, not inaccurately.

"You can say that again," muttered Winters as we walked out into the bright winter noon.

I had one more errand to do, one which particularly mystified Winters; then we drove back to the house.

No one was in sight when we got there and I was suddenly afraid that the whole lot had fled; the presence of four detectives in grey business suits reassured me; the situation was under control.

Winters and I sat in the drawing-room drinking Martinis; at least I drank several and he tasted one. I found I was still groggy from the sleeping pills and needed the stimulant or depressant of alcohol, whichever it is. I also needed a bit of courage for the evening ahead. I was like an actor preparing for a crucial first night. I couldn't afford to muff a line.

We chatted about one thing and the other, both growing more excited by the minute . . . he against his will, too, since he disapproved of what I was doing and would have, if it had been possible, stopped me right then and there and concluded the case on his own more pedestrian lines.

At five o'clock Miss Flynn called with the information I had requested. I thanked her profusely; she had, in that inexorable way of hers, found out more than I should have thought possible. "Nevertheless, Mr. Sargeant, bearing in mind these Revelations, I would conduct myself with Extreme Caution." I assured her that I would.

"All the evidence is now at hand, buddy," I said, patting Winters on the back, feeling very content and a little drunk.

"It had better be," said the policeman solemnly, eating the onion which I had put in his Martini.

3

There was no doubt in anyone's mind that evening that something extraordinary was going to happen.

Everyone was studiedly casual at table. Ledbetter told a few old-time political stories and there was a great deal of merry laughter. I sat next to Walter Langdon and we discussed politics and journalism.

"The theme of the demagogue," I said, weightly, "seems particularly fascinating to American writers. I suppose because we have so few of them in this country."

"You mean so few *effective* ones." Of them all Langdon was perhaps the most relaxed, in appearance.

"Well, yes. The great modern example was Huey Long. I suspect a hundred novels and plays will be written about him before the century's over."

"Penn Warren did a pretty thorough job," said Langdon.

"I always liked the book Don Passos wrote better. You remember? It was called *Number One.*"

Langdon nodded. "I read it. I think I've read everything about Long ever written."

"I've been told he had a good chance of becoming President."

"A lot of people thought it might happen, God help us. Fortunately God did and he was assassinated."

" 'Killed in the shell', as it were."

Langdon looked startled; he smiled. "Yes, that's one way of putting it."

"Your way, or rather Shakespeare's."

"The theme of my piece for the *Advanceguard,* too."

"I thought you were going to show it to me."

"You can see it any time you like. I'm taking it back with me tomorrow. I got it all done, first draft, that is . . . thanks to your typewriter paper."

"Think nothing of it. Is it thus always with tyrants?"

"Not always . . . if only it were."

"We should have a much better world, I suspect."

Langdon nodded, his eyes suddenly bright. "If only people would act in time they could save the world so much pain. But they're weak, afraid to take the life of one man for fear of losing their own."

"But you would risk yours, wouldn't you?"

"Oh yes," said Langdon quietly, "I would."

When dinner was over we went into the drawing-room, as was the custom of the house, for coffee. Winters kept trying to catch my eye for some sign but I gave him none. I was in no hurry. Timing was important at this stage.

I was standing off at one end of the room observing the dinner guests and witnesses-to-be when Roger Pomeroy came over and said: "I'm afraid I was very indiscreet the other night . . . must've been tight . . . didn't realise I'd told you all I had."

"It's perfectly all right," I said.

"Do wish you would keep what I said in strictest confidence, no matter what happens. Verbena was furious with me for telling you about that contract she arranged. She's afraid you're going to write it up in the papers."

"Not a chance,' I said amiably. "I don't even think it'll come out at the trial."

"Trial?"

"Tell her I'm not really a newspaper-man, that I'm not down here to try and ferret out scandals for the delight of the people. All I'm interested in is the murders."

"Oh." Pomeroy looked at me blankly. "Well, don't get me in Dutch with her, will you? That contract could be misunderstood, you know. Perfectly legal and all that but you know what a stink those people like Pearson make when the find out that a friend has done another friend a good turn, all perfectly on the up and up."

I allowed that I knew just how it was. I could see he was uneasy but I gave him no more assurances. Then I strolled over to Mrs. Rhodes. She was sitting by the silver coffee-pot, pouring, as she had done the night before and every night, doubtless, for many years. I sat down beside her.

"It is very hard," I said.

She looked away, her face set. "Will you have more coffee?" she asked mechanically.

"No thank you." The thought of coffee made me ill. I had tasted it all day: the result of that stomach pump.

"You are going to go through with this?" She did not look at me as she spoke; her hand toyed with the silver sugar-tongs.

"I must."

Before she could speak, Camilla Pomeroy was upon us. "I couldn't've been more horrified!" she said, her eyes wide. "I just found out from Mr. Winters what really happened . . . and with *my* sleeping pills, too, or rather Roger's only we keep them in my vanity-case. Someone came in yesterday and took the whole bottle. They must've emptied it all in your cup last night. Though how, I don't know, since Mrs. Rhodes was the one who poured." Then, as though alarmed at the implications of what she had said, she began to talk very fast. "Thank heavens, though, you're all right today. A third tragedy would have been more than flesh could bear."

"Well, I have a strong stomach."

"You must have. Of course I've always hated the idea of having sleeping pills around, especially those strong ones Roger takes. They could knock out an elephant in no time at all. I think they're an absolute menace."

"A menace," repeated Mrs. Rhodes absently.

Across the room Ellen signalled to me. I excused myself and joined her at the backgammon-table.

"Are you really going to be a sleuth?" she asked, setting up the board.

"I suppose so."

"What fun! You take the greens; I'll take the whites."

"For chastity?"

"Don't be rude." We set up our boards. I watched Mrs.

203

Rhodes across the room; she seemed distracted. Her hands nervously touched objects: silver, china, the jewels at her throat, as though she were trying to satisfy herself that the world was real, that this was not all a dream.

Langdon sat talking quietly to Ledbetter, discussing politics, no doubt. Every now and then Langdon looked over at us, at me; if he was anxious he did not betray it. Verbena Pruitt sat like a colossus between the Pomeroys who chattered loudly across her, talking of Talisman City. She ignored them, as though they were chattering birds come to rest upon her monumental self. Her eyes had a vacant, faraway look. Soon. Soon. Soon.

Ellen was off to a good start with double sixes.

We played in silence for several minutes. I watched the room, aware that Winters had a man at each door and another out on the street by the windows. Winters himself pretended to read a magazine.

"Well, it'll soon be over," said Ellen, shaking her dice.

"Will you be glad?"

"Lord yes? Though I've missed Bess Pringle's party because of your silly sleeping pills."

"Bess Pringle gives a lot of parties."

"I know but I wanted particularly to go to this one."

I picked up one of her men. She swore softly. She rolled but couldn't come in. "Peter dear, who did it? Tell me. I'm dying to know."

"You did, my love."

She rolled her dice and came in on a four and picked up my man. Her face had not changed expression. "What a horrid thing to say, even as a joke."

"What a horrid thing to do, even as a joke. It's all right with me if you want to kill your father and Rufus but I think it ever so unfriendly to try and knock off your fiancé. It shows a lack of sensitivity."

Ellen smiled, her old dazzling smile. "You're going to have a hard time proving it, my lamb," she said, her voice pitched so that only I could hear.

"It's already proven. I spent the day getting evidence."

"And?"

All my men were in home place; I began to take them off. "When you were a small and wicked girl you were engaged to be married to Verbena's nephew. At the last minute that passion of yours for forbidden vice made you run off with a gymnast. Your father caught you and brought you back home. He had the marriage annulled and you hated him for it. When you were old enough, you left home for good."

"Ancient history," said Ellen, unperturbed.

"Ancient, yes, but we must construct a motive carefully. There is a great deal of proof that you hated your father for other reasons; this particular interference is good enough for a start. About a year ago he tried to get you to go into a hospital for observation. When you refused, he reduced your allowance; he also threatened to have you committed. You came down here a month ago to talk to him abouut it. While you were here you learned, probably by accident, about his business dealings with Hollister. The first thought which went through your head was to blackmail your father into giving you more money. It is possible that you *did* get something out of him . . . we'll find that out by checking your bank. In any case, you were aware of the papers that he had drawn up, implicating Rufus in the company scandal and clearing himself . . ."

"There's an awful lot of guesswork in this," said Ellen.

"There has to be when it comes to a complicated motive. Fortunately, there is no guesswork in what happened afterwards. On the spur of the moment you came to Washington, full of a desperate plan. I'm sure that you didn't arrive with any intention of killing your father: talk, however, of the new Pomeroy explosive did the trick. It looked like a perfect set-up: your father is killed and his enemy Pomeroy is suspected: all very convenient.

"The first part worked beautifully, but then the complications began, proving no doubt that murders should not be committed on such short notice. Verbena Pruitt told you and your mother that Pomeroy had a perfect alibi, that he could be proven motiveless at a moment's notice. So you had to act quickly. Rufus Hollister seemed like the next best possibility. You had access to the papers which implicated him in the business tangle; all you had to do was, strategically and while the heat was still on Pomeroy, direct suspicion towards Rufus . . . and it was here that your troubles really began. In the last few hours I have tried to figure how you might have done it differently; you will be pleased to know that your method was about the best I could think of, though of course it wasn't good enough."

"I think I'd like a drink," she said thoughtfully, rolling two and one.

"Later. You wrote me a very whimsical note which, if I'd been quicker, I should have spotted as being vintage Ellen. You directed my attention to Rufus Hollister, knowing that I would follow the lead, that I would also pass it on to the police. You were also in possession of the papers, having the night before assaulted a plain-clothes man, looted the library and sent me, on the return visit to your room, hurtling through space, a bit of predatory behaviour I find in the worst taste."

"I'll have Scotch," said Ellen.

"You are deliberately trying to diminish my one great moment," I said irritably.

"Well, if this proves to be your one great moment, all I can say is . . ."

"Shut up. You went, the night before I got the letter, to the study and took down a copy of the *Congressional Record* in which you, or perhaps your father in your presence, had hidden documents which, if certain affairs came to light, would be executed, absolving the Senator of guilt. You then make a mistake. You left the copy of the *Record* in your bedroom where I saw it, and, though I must admit I didn't quite get the point the first time I saw it, I realised later that it could only have come from your father's study, and since you had not the faintest interest in politics and since all the papers had been cleared out of the study, this volume must, in some way then, be connected with the Hollister papers."

She grunted; she kept on playing, though, rolling the dice and moving her men mechanically. I continued to take mine off as I talked.

"So, then, you had the papers and suspicion was cast, rather cleverly, on Rufus even before the Pomeroy alibi was known to either me or the police. I suggest if you had left it at that, you might have got off. I suppose you lost your head. The case against Pomeroy was due to fall apart any minute. Even though you had cast suspicion on Hollister, you weren't satisfied that that would be enough. So, instead of letting me chase the papers you sent the papers to chase me . . . and, incidentally, it was that phrase which first set me moving in the right direction. Do you know why?"

"No, and I don't want to hear."

"I shall tell you, anyway," I said serenely. "Your mother, by accident, used it to me a few minutes after I had got the letter, making me think *she* had written the letter. Later, when I was fairly sure she had not written it, it occurred

207

to me in a flash of purest inspiration that a paper-chase was an old children's game which she had doubtless played and which she had taught her daughter. In other words, it was a family reference so immediate as to be common to you both."

"Oh, for Christ's sake!" she exploited scornfully. "I can't bear this on an empty stomach. Get me a drink or I'll get it myself."

"Not yet. But that will not be a part of the case . . . I just thought you might be interested in how a superior mind can proceed through semantic association to a correct deduction." I paused for some outcry, but she went on playing, scornfully. "Now the plot moves quickly. You decide Hollister must commit suicide. You toy with the idea of forcing him into it by threatening him with exposure. But this won't work. You telephone him at the office while I am there and you make a date to meet at midnight, in his room, implying no doubt that you have the papers, knowing he is terrified they may fall into the hands of the police. You keep that date, collecting en route your mother's pistol you used to play with as a girl, shooting targets in the back yard."

"I thought we were all at the Chevy Chase Club that night?"

"All but you; from eleven-thirty to twelve-thirty you were occupied not with that muscular Marine officer, but with the murder of Rufus Hollister. You took a taxi home. You slipped in that unguarded side entrance which you unwisely told me about later. You waited, no doubt in the hall, until Ledbetter stormed out of Hollister's room and then you marched in, shot him with that remarkably quiet pistol, typed a confession at great speed, left the house by the same way you entered, hailed a cab and rejoined Langdon at the Club. Total time elapsed: one hour."

"Very fanciful."

"This afternoon I paid a visit to the taxicab company where, I am happy to say, you were identified after three hours of rather discouraging confusion."

Only a sharp intake of breath indicated I had scored at last.

"Yesterday, when I had my talk with Mrs. Rhodes and announced (inaccurately, you will be sad to hear) that I knew who the murderer was, you were listening in the hall. In that direct way of yours you determined that *my* suicide was definitely in order, the sooner the better."

"Prove I was in the hall."

"Just a bit of circumstantial evidence. I heard someone run up the stairs. A few minutes later I went up myself; I got a strong whiff of your perfume."

She chuckled softly. "Sherlock Holmes by a nose. I'd like to hear *that* in a court."

"You won't, though you'll hear other things. I am merely trying to give you an intimate view of the way my mind works. You will have to listen to so much dull evidence that I thought I would treat you to those fine little points . . ."

She told me what I could do with those fine little points as I rolled doubles and took my last three men off the board. The game was over.

"Fortunately, you will not be executed, for which I am thankful, despite the heartless way you tried to murder me. You will be removed to a private institution where you will spend the remainder of your life weaving baskets and causing no end of trouble for the other inmates."

"What do you mean?" Her lips had tightened in a thin red line; her eyes were large and dangerously bright.

"I mean, Ellen, that after the court consults with that middle-aged analyst of yours, Dr. Breitbach, whom you only partly conquered, you will be declared criminally insane, which you are, and committed for the rest of your unnatural days."

"You son of a bitch," said Ellen Rhodes, throwing her dice in my face.

4

The story was all mine, and I made the most of it.

The Pomeroys returned to Talisman City, and, I assume, barring an occasional excursion on Camilla's part into extramarital situations, lived a contented and exemplary life, manufacturing munitions.

Verbena Pruitt, untouched by scandal, proceeded to deliver the women's vote to a successful candidate for President, for which she was rewarded with the Bureau of Fisheries and a private car and chauffeur.

Johnson Ledbetter was allowed to take his seat in the Senate, though everyone deplored the necessity of seating him for several days. But now his pronouncements on the economic structure of the nation are taken with great seriousness; he is already on the Committee of Spoils and Patronage. His nephew is employed as his private secretary, while his niece draws a considerable salary as a typist in his office, a task for which she has demonstrated a remarkable skill, since she lives in Talisman City, her salary being collected *in absentia* by the Senator.

Mrs. Rhodes conducted herself with great dignity during the trial, which was mercifully short. No family skeletons were rattled in public and the court speedily brought in a decision that the defendant was indeed paranoiac, placing her for life in a shady institution in Maryland, where she would receive the best of care.

I did not appear in court. My testimony was handled by the prosecutor, and though I should have liked the glory it was wisest, all things considered, to let it fall upon the sturdy shoulders of Lieutenant Winters, whose photograph appeared in the papers many times during the week, giving him an illusion of celebrity which the passage of time, I knew, would dispel. He had had his moment, though.

I had mine when the *Globe* hit the street the following afternoon with the exclusive story. We had beaten every paper in town and my intimate descriptions of the murderess at bay were very fine. The sort of thing which ordinarily would have broken Ellen up with laughter.

Walter Langdon and I went back on the train to New York together, and he allowed me to read the first draft of his study in political murder. I thought it very fine and suggested he make an epic poem of it. He did not take this kindly, but I was quite serious: there hasn't been a decent narrative poet since Byron.

I had moments of remorse when I thought of Ellen in that insane asylum. It had been, after all, no business of mine. I would have dropped the whole thing if she hadn't tried to kill me, which, I thought, had been carrying her rôle as the Lucrezia Borgia of Massachusetts Avenue too far. We had been, after all, fond of each other.

Two weeks later, just before the poodle's recital at Town Hall, I met Mrs. Goldmountain backstage. It was the first time I had seen her since Washington, since the trial.

She rushed up to me. She was magnificently dressed, with a diamond butterfly in her hair and gold-dust sprinkled over her eyelids.

"I couldn't be more nervous!" she said, clutching my hands.

"There's no cause for alarm," I said calmly. "We've got the whole show under control. I've been in consultation with Heigh-Ho all week. We have television cameras in the lobby to televise the celebrities, *Look* to take photographs, and all the news services are represented; nothing can go wrong."

"I hope not. Hermione has been practising like mad these last two weeks. Oh, we *can't* let her down."

She twisted a bit of black lace nervously between her fingers. "Alma Edderdale is here, and I asked Margaret Truman especially to come. There's to be a whole train-load of Washington people." Photographers, news-men, officials of Heigh-Ho pushed by us. There was a great racket. From where we stood in the wings we could see the stage and part of the house: it was nearly filled already.

"Oh, by the way, how clever you were about the Ellen Rhodes thing. Who would have thought it? And according to everyone, *you* worked it all out."

"Just luck," I said quietly.

"I'm sure it was more than that. You know I went over to Maryland to see her yesterday."

"Who? Ellen?"

"Certainly. I was always very fond of her. I thought I'd go and console her . . . nasty girl."

"What did she do?"

"Do! She barked at me and pretended she was a dog!" Ellen Victrix, I thought . . . the ending was not so unhappy after all. I pitied the younger doctors.

But then Hermione, wearing a black velvet bow decorated with seed pearls, was led past us. Mrs. Goldmountain gave her a parting hug.

There was loud applause when she appeared on stage with her accompanist.

A moment later the piano broke into one of the very grandest arias from *Norma* and Hermione's voice, unearthly and loud, floated in the air.

Her subsequent stardom in nine movies is known to all; after the ninth she lost her voice and was forced to make personal appearances until the grim reaper laid her low. Her Town Hall debut was a public relations success, though artistically her press was mixed. Virgil Thomson in the *Herald Tribune* summed up the general view when he said that her voice was a small one and not well trained; nevertheless, despite her unreadiness, he found her stage presence utterly beguiling and her graciousness, especially during the curtain calls, remarkable.

Also available from
The Armchair Detective Library

Death in the Fifth Position by Edgar Box
Spider Kiss by Harlan Ellison
The Shakeout by Ken Follett
The Bear Raid by Ken Follett
Dead Cert by Dick Francis
Nerve by Dick Francis
For Kicks by Dick Francis
Odds Against by Dick Francis
Licence to Kill by John Gardner
The November Man by Bill Granger
The Blessing Way by Tony Hillerman
The Fly on the Wall by Tony Hillerman
Johnny Havoc by John Jakes
Havoc for Sale by John Jakes
Holiday for Havoc by John Jakes
The Big Bounce by Elmore Leonard
Hombre by Elmore Leonard
Rosemary's Baby by Ira Levin
The Scarlatti Inheritance by Robert Ludlum
Cop Hater by Ed McBain
The Mugger by Ed McBain
The Pusher by Ed McBain
First Blood by David Morrell
Crocodile on the Sandbank by Elizabeth Peters
The Curse of the Pharaohs by Elizabeth Peters

A Prospect of Vengeance by Anthony Price

Collector Edition $25 Limited Edition $75
(100 copies, signed, and slipcased)
Postage & handling $3/book, 50¢ each additional

A trade edition with library binding is also available.
Please contact us for price and ordering information.